IT WAS LIKE EVERYTHING THAT HAPPENED
HAD FROZE ME . . . .

When he started to talk you could hear how tears was trapped in his throat. I felt like I wanted to touch him, but I couldn't. I couldn't cause I was afraid I would hit him again.

Oakley Brownhouse swallowed his tears and went, His name was Gil and he's dead, okay? He's dead.

ALSO BY ADAM RAPP

THE BUFFALO TREE

MISSING THE PIANO

I

THE BODYBOXES

They're burning tires in the Pits again. I can't see them cause I'm hided, but I can smell them all thick and hot and fiery like pepper and smoke and wet thunderhorses mixed together. Tick Burrowman says the tires look like little halos floating in the dark, like some angels is lost in all that blackness. Tick Burrowman says burning tires keeps the fishflies away.

The Digit Kids is down there busting rocks. You can hear their splittingpicks going ballistic like little blasterguns popping off far far away, like in some place you read about in a story. Shale Bluehouse is down there. Shale's my best friend and we was both Bluehouse kids at the Holy Family Agency and we used to give each other pens and paperclips and other stuff we'd find, but now he's down in the Pits busting rocks with all the other Digit Kids. Murl Greenhouse and Spider Brownhouse is down there too, but Murl and Spider don't make me sad the way Shale does cause they was always poking you with forks and sitting on you and stuff. Whenever I hear the splittingpicks I picture Shale and it makes the muscles in my chest feel funny.

If you listen real careful you can hear the ditch dogs, too. You can hear them barking through their muzzlestraps. The

Syndicate trains the ditch dogs to hunt the Undertwelves and the Elders. Sometimes their barks sound like the rocks getting busted and you can't tell what's rocks and what's ditch dogs, but it don't bother you too much if Tick Burrowman's singing a song or cleaning trees or having you wash water with him. It don't bother you too much if there's closer noises that's bigger than the barks.

They'll make you a Digit Kid if you're a Undertwelve and you ain't taller than the Future Stick. The Future Stick's made out of metal and it's got this little edge at the top and if your head don't touch it they'll send you right to the Numbering Line. They'll send you to the Numbering Line if you got something wrong with you like a limp or a small hand, too. And if you slump or got bad teeth you might as well walk right over and give them your shoulder so they can start drawing that digit.

When a line of Digit Kids goes down into the Pits, you don't never see them come back up. Tick Burrowman says he's seen a couple of Digit Kids running all lost and swervy through the Bone Trees. He says he tried talking to them, too, but they just runned away like little lopsided ghosts. I ain't seen no Digit Kids running up out of the Pits. I ain't seen nothing like that.

If you get through the Bone Trees then you got to cross the Red River and if you cross the Red River you'll come to the Forsaken Lawn. The Forsaken Lawn's like a gazillion miles long, and on the other side is Toptown. No one really knows what Toptown is, but they talk about it the way they used to talk about birthdays and Christmas when birthdays and Christmas still meant something. They say Toptown's where the Creature Clouds stop and the Sun starts shining regular again.

There's sixteen minimonths now. There used to be twelve regular months, but all that changed after the Creature Clouds came. Tick Burrowman says it's cause the Moon croaked. He says the calendar makers from the Syndicate measure a month by the amount of light the Moon can make. And now it's like the Moon ain't even *there* no more, so they double the days and cut the weeks in half. There's two doubledays in a halfweek and two halfweeks in a minimonth.

It's been raining sixty-three doubledays straight. At forty-nine they thought it would stop. They thought it would stop at fifty-four too but it didn't.

Sometimes you think the rain's going to stop cause you can hear how it slows on the front of the life hole, but then it starts up again like it was just resting cause it got tired. Sometimes it sounds like little people running around. Like they're running around cause they can't find something they lost. Even though I'm in the back with the bodyboxes I can still hear the rain.

Tick Burrowman was cleaning trees on his planing table when Second Staff Brown came ducking through the front. Second Staff Brown's with the Syndicate and when he walks you can hear stuff jangling in his pockets.

There's this little hole in my bodybox where the wood went

bad. You can look through the hole and under the curtain, but all you see is legs and feet. Legs and feet and Syndicate boots and the bottom of Second Staff Brown's greatcoat sweeping over the floor like a big falcon tail.

Second Staff Brown's got these pointy soles on his boots that look like burnt lion teeth. They're all white from the quickdust and if you stare at them too long it's like they don't got no legs or manparts attached to them. It's like they can roar at you by themselves.

Second Staff Brown comes up to check the bodyboxes and he's always drinking a glass of washed water from Tick Burrowman's sinkwell. If you don't wash the water you can get this thing called Blackfrost that will croak you in four days. It don't matter to Second Staff Brown that me and Tick Burrowman put all that time into boiling the rot out so we can have some clean water for later. Even though he don't know nothing about me—about how Tick Burrowman's hiding a Undertwelve in his life hole, and a *girl* Undertwelve at that— it don't matter to Second Staff Brown. To him it's like Tick Burrowman ain't really there, even though he says nice things to him and puts that music in his voice.

Second Staff Brown drinks the washed water and stomps his boots again and you can see rain jumping off the toetips. You can smell the boot polish and when you smell it you know he'll ask Tick Burrowman how many bodyboxes he's joined and how many he's planed and how many can he get out by the end of the doubleday. And you know he'll pull out his little notepad and make some marks, and then he'll flip the top with one hand and slide it back into the pocket of his greatcoat like it's something he can do in his *sleep*. Then he'll ask Tick Burrowman about how many bodyboxes he thinks he can push through his life hole by next Oldsunday when Astan Loe comes clopping to the Shelf on his big thunderhorse.

Astan Loe comes to the Shelf to collect stuff. He runs the Syndicate and you see his picture on trees and telephone poles and the sides of all the old buildings that still got sides. He's got these mean eyes that look like smeared bulletholes, and he's got this big honking black mustache that looks like he's had it ever since he was a little *kid*. It's funny how you don't never see no one painting his picture; it just appears all big and spooky-looking like *God* put it there or something.

On one Oldsunday Astan Loe made everyone give up their forks, knives, and spoons. He let Tick Burrowman keep a spoon cause you got to have a spoon to eat the mush that the Syndicate drops off every Oldmonday. The mush tastes like water and cornslop, but it's better than nothing. Sometimes you can just hold the spoon on your tongue and it feels good cause the metal in it makes your mouth cold.

After he took the silverware, Astan Loe came for tin cans and paperclips. Then it was belt buckles and coat buttons.

Last minimonth it was paper. When him and his Syndicate men bundled and stacked and carted it off in the collection wagon, Tick Burrowman said Astan Loe turnt his big thunderhorse around and announced that on the final Oldsunday of next minimonth he would be back for aluminum foil.

Tick Burrowman says aluminum foil's important cause it don't rust. So he had me take all of the aluminum scraps out of his cupboard in the kitchencove and make a ball with it and now that ball is sitting all small and lonesome in the middle of a busted chair in the room where I sleep. Every night when I lay in my halfbed I stare at it and it's like I'm staring at a little silver planet and it's like I'm on that planet and it's spinning away from here. Sometimes I pretend that Shale Bluehouse is on that planet too, and we're like telling jokes and waving to the stars and stuff.

Second Staff Brown blows into his fists and talks about the wind and how it's pushing the rain. He always starts talking to Tick Burrowman about the rain. He talks about the rain even before he says hello.

Tick Burrowman's like, Hello, Second Staff Brown. Hello, hello.

Godawful, flyforsaken rain.

It ain't gettin no better, that's for sure.

Like it's got a will of its own. How you doin, Tick?

Oh, pretty fair, pretty fair.

You can hear how they're kind of shaking hands or maybe just patting each other on the shoulder and nodding.

Second Staff Brown goes, It weren't so bad when it was

fallin regular. Just piddlin on your head and rollin off your shoulderboards. Mother Nature's little conniption fit.

Tick Burrowman's like, I know it, Second Staff Brown. I know it.

It's hard enough dealin with all that business in the Pits.

Can't imagine.

Little fellas howlin like that. Goin to a knee like they's already old. And girlies, too.

Must be hard.

Awful hard, Tick. Awful awful hard.

I know it is, Tick Burrowman says in his old rusty voice. He says *I know it is* a lot to Second Staff Brown. It's like saying it makes them better friends.

Second Staff Brown takes another long step and sweeps something off his pants. You can hear how his boots is killing the floor.

He goes, It don't even look right.

Tick Burrowman's like, The rain or that business in the Pits?

Well, the rain, Tick.

No, it don't look right, Second Staff Brown. It shore don't.

Don't look like rain, that's for sure. And you can just call me Brown, Tick. Or Browny. You should know that by now.

Well.

We don't got to be formal when we're here in the life hole.

If you say so.

They're quiet for a minute and you can hear Second Staff

Brown fiddling in his pockets again. I think about what kinds of things he's got, like some keys and a lighter and maybe some of the old money you find sometimes; like he's rubbing two of those pennycoppers together, the same way Shale Bluehouse always does for luck. Shale says the man on the pennycopper's called Angryham Lincoln and that he was the president of the United States like a gazillion years ago.

Never seen nothing like this rain, Second Staff Brown says. Not a thing.

The rain will burn you unless you've been rubbed down with the safe jam. It looks like busted apples and smells like a fish on fire, but the safe jam keeps the rain from burning your skin. Before Tick Burrowman goes outside to drag trees, he always rubs it on his arms and on his face and on the back of his neck. You can see when he misses a spot cause of the blisters.

They don't say nothing for a long time and you can hear the rain on the front of the life hole. It sounds like something boiling in a pot.

Hiding's a good time to pull out my nest. It's smaller than my hand and there was this little blue egg in it when I finded it in the Bone Trees. For a while I kept waiting for a baby chicken to bust out of it, but it didn't never come. One doubleday it cracked, but the only thing that came out was this boogery-looking stuff. I left the egg alone after that, but I accidentally crushed it when I tried to kill this spider that was trying to steal that boogery stuff. I still keep the shell parts for luck. They don't move too much cause they're stuck in the sticks.

When I look at my nest it makes me think of Shale and all the things we was going to do before the Syndicate came and clinched everyone at the Holy Family Agency. Like how we was going to go looking for lost cats and make little plastic raincoats and shoes for them and stuff like that.

Second Staff Brown clears his throat and goes, How many canisters you got through today, Old Timer?

It's funny how Second Staff Brown calls the bodyboxes *canisters*.

Tick Burrowman's like, How many you need, Browny?

As many as we can get our hands on, Tickyman. Them little ones is pilin up down there. Pilin up like so much forgotten laundry. Never seen heaps of kids like that before.

Sounds mighty sad, Browny.

And the smell, godawmighty, Tick.

Can't even imagine.

Hits you like a door closin in your face.

Don't know how you all manage what's goin on down there.

Difficult times take difficult measures.

Tick Burrowman don't say nothing after that. Him and Second Staff Brown stay quiet for a minute and you can hear the wind crying through the cracks in the door.

After a minute Tick Burrowman's like, You still catchin them little ones runnin outta the Pits?

Oh, once in a while. Not too many, though. It ain't that easy, Tickyman. They got the Pits to get through. All the fellas tendin to em. Keepin dibs and such. And then there's the ditch dogs. We got them hounds trained up real well. Then if they get through them they got the wall to climb. And with the rain slickin it up, that rock ladder ain't no picnic.

I spose it ain't, Browny. Spose it ain't.

Him and Second Staff Brown is quiet again. Then Tick Burrowman goes, Well, I got through twelve bodyboxes this mornin, Browny.

Twelve's a durn sturdy number, Tick.

I do what I can.

Seems like you been pickin up the pace a bit lately.

Well, joinin them boards is gettin a little swifter. Used to smart up my hands but you get used to it.

Speed and volume. That's what we're about, Tick. You make em and I pick em, pack em, and send em on down. Good old-fashioned teamwork.

Two fellas ridin a teamwork train.

Choo choo, here we come!

Stoke the engine, ride the line!

They laugh and it sounds like four or five men laughing cause you don't never hear no one laughing in the life hole. Then Tick Burrowman starts coughing and then he's stomping his foot and cursing. They stop laughing cause of how Tick Burrowman's cough turns ugly. Sometimes it sounds like his lungbags is made out of paper and that paper's getting ripped with forks and knives. He coughs and curses the Creature Clouds and clears his throat and says, Scuse me.

You can hear Second Staff Brown walking to the sinkwell to get Tick Burrowman a glass of washed water. Tick Burrowman says Thanks. You can hear Tick Burrowman wrestling with that cough and sucking the air and slowing himself so he can drink the water. His throat glurps when he drinks, like something getting pulled out of the mud.

Second Staff Brown's like, Get your wind, Old Timer, get your wind, now.

Tick Burrowman's breathing regular again and after he clears his throat one last time they go quiet. The rain sounds like it got scared and went away but it didn't.

Second Staff Brown is smoking now and you can smell the cigarette all sweet and thick and burny. He pops the top of his lighter a few times and goes, Them trees Joe Painter been choppin good enough for you?

I'd say they're pretty fair.

Poplars, are they?

They mighta been them once. Now they're all maligned, Browny. Maligned and awfully meager. Cleanin em's the tough stuff.

Durn knotty timber.

Can't scrape every fishfly.

Fishflies fishflies. Them hellified things keep jumpin outta the river. Jumpin like nothing I ever seen before.

I heard you all torched em up pretty fair last time.

Second Staff Brown's like, Yep, yep, and smokes and blows it through his nose so it sounds like a snake trying to talk. Then he says, That Joe Painter's a good kid.

Lucky boy to be gettin in with you Syndicate fellas at such a age.

We know how to pick em, Tickyman. I can spot a Futurist right in the Numbering Line.

And how's that, Browny?

Oh, just certain signs is all. Strong back. Clean teeth. Good shine in his eye. Let the weak ones go. Keep the strong ones for the future. Sometimes we'll ask one of the younger ones to drop and give us some old-fashioned pushups. They hit twinny they might find themselves with a pretty decent bit of tomorrow.

Twinny pushups, huh?

That's right. Keep the strong ones. Let the weak go. Kinda like fishin.

I think of Shale and how he was slumping in the line when we was counting off. I think that maybe he would have been pulled from the line if he stood up straighter when they was looking us over. He could have been a *Futurist* if he hided his leg better. I think of that and it makes me feel small inside.

Like I got doll parts instead of guts in my stomach.

Tick Burrowman goes, How old is that young Joe Painter fella, anyhow?

Fifteen, sixteen.

Fresh legs on that one.

Fresh as a thunderhorse.

Dog*gone* fresh legs.

Second Staff Brown smokes and goes, Must be hard choppin down a tree, ain't it, Tick?

You got the right sort of hatchetaxe and a good strumf in your back it ain't too stodgy . . .

Tick Burrowman has to stop so he can cough and spit and then goes, I've seen more than a few sturdy men take a knee and clutch at their hearts.

Second Staff Brown don't say nothing after that and I think maybe he don't say nothing cause he's picturing what Tick Burrowman said, like in his mind he can see some *Digit Kid* going down with his splittingpick clutched to his side and he can hear his heart busting the same way a clock busts if you throw it against the wall.

You can hear the Creature Clouds dragging thunder. It sounds like a bunch of bears lost in a cave. When it ends, Second Staff Brown smokes some more and Tick Burrowman goes, Draggin them trees in ain't no picnic, I'll tell you that.

Second Staff Brown's like, You need some help you just let me know.

Oh, no, I do fine by myself.

Tick Burrowman's old and his hair is yellow and kind of no color in some places and he's got a face like wet paper and his eyes look sad but they ain't sad like crying. They're sad like he's thinking or praying. They're sad like the weather is sad. Whenever he goes outside he wears a black garbage bag over his clothes. He always looks lonesome when he comes back in. It's like there's something on the other side of his life hole that he lost and ain't never going to find again.

Second Staff Brown goes, If you don't mind me sayin, you look a little rundown, Tick.

Just the backaches is all.

That clutchincough of yours don't exactly sound like a Christmas carol.

Oh, that old thing ain't nothin but a bad habit.

You keep yourself warm, now.

Oh, I do, Browny, I do. We get a good windy fire goin in here.

We?

What's that?

You said We.

Oh, that's just a figger of speech, Browny. I, me, we. Me myself and I, that sorta thing. Three Ticks in the kitchencove.

Huh.

That's all I meant, Browny.

They don't say nothing for a minute and then Second Staff

Brown goes, That's funny.

Tick Burrowman's like, What's funny?

Well, for a second I kinda pictured someone else in here with you. Some ladyfriend to help with the chores and such.

Been a long stretch since those days. A long, lonely stretch, Browny.

I could request a Futurist for you.

Oh, no thanks, Browny, I do fine by myself.

One Futurist just to help you drag them poplars. All I gotta do is fill out a form.

No, no, too much pride for that. Too much pride.

In your time I'm sure you would've made quite an impression on the Syndicate. Hard worker like you.

In my time there *wasn't* no Syndicate, Browny.

Well, you're right about that.

No Syndicate. No Creature Clouds neither. Flying Fox was somethin you rode in for fun.

The Syndicate lets Tick Burrowman stay in his life hole and they don't take him away in the Flying Fox with all the other Elders, and along with the Oldmonday mush they give him blocks of cheese and boxes of milk powder. He asks for extras cause of me, but he don't tell them that. He just tells them that he's got a tapeworm and that the tapeworm keeps eating half the food he eats and they sometimes laugh cause he's so skinny and old, but they always give him the extras anyway. All he's got to do is keep making bodyboxes.

Second Staff Brown walks around a little and goes, How's that tapeworm, Tick?

Oh, she's still down low stoppin up my tubes. Thievin like a wolf in a meadow. As ornery as ever.

Never knew a man so frail to eat so much.

It's sinful, Browny, it really is.

Well, you earn it.

I might try to draw her out.

How's that, Tick?

Well, all you need is some good chicken broth and a pot of beans. Wag your tongue over the bowl and she'll come wigglin through right as the rain is gray.

That right?

Right as the rain is gray, Browny.

So I spose you're askin for some good chicken broth and a pot of beans.

Old bellybird'll march right out.

Hup, two, three, four.

I'll wrastle her to the floor and strangle the everlovin wind outta her.

Second Staff Brown laughs and says, I'll see what I can do, Tickyman. I'll see what I can do.

And I thank you for it, Browny.

Tick Burrowman's knees wobble and stick and you know that underneath his pants his legs is old and crooked like some goat bones. Second Staff Brown's legs is thick and strong-looking with his Syndicate slacks all clean and creased. Now four legs is walking toward me. They keep getting bigger and bigger like someone's blowing air into them.

The slip curtain gets pulled and now Tick Burrowman and Second Staff Brown is in the back. I can smell them the way you can smell something that won't wash off your hand.

You can't even describe the way a man smells. Sometimes it's a scary smell and sometimes it's a smell that makes you angry.

I don't think I would like being a man cause they get too hairy. Once I seen a man who had so much hair he looked like a boogywolf. I ain't never seen no real boogywolf but Shale Bluehouse seen one once and he said it had so much hair you couldn't even see its *teeth*. And then when men get old they get real skinny and lose all that hair and wind up looking like bald turkeys.

Second Staff Brown bends down to fix his bootstrap and through the hole I can see how his face is long and smooth and if you didn't know he was with the Syndicate you would think he was nice. You can imagine a man like Second Staff Brown with a baby cause of his face and sometimes his voice loses that metal and makes you feel safe. But once you start imagining his boots and his pants and all those black buttons on his greatcoat, that baby disappears so fast it's like he dropped it in the *Pits*.

Tick Burrowman and Second Staff Brown grunt and stack the bodyboxes and push the wheely board to the front of the life hole. Their mansmells is thick now.

I think of those tires burning like little halos down in the Pits. I picture the Digit Kids with their splittingpicks and I think of Shale Bluehouse and how he carries those two pennycoppers in his pocket and how he's always rubbing them together and talking about Angryham Lincoln like he's going to give him some luck. I think about that and it makes me feel small again.

When their legs go away I start to breathe. I am hot and my face itches. Tick Burrowman and Second Staff Brown say goodbye and pat each other on the shoulder.

Tick Burrowman's coughing again. He wrestles with his lungpuddles and curses the Creature Clouds and stomps his foot. That cough was so ugly I think it had a color. I think it was black and brown and blue.

As soon as Second Staff Brown leaves with his twelve new bodyboxes, I will see Tick Burrowman's goat legs walking back here again, looking old and a little crooked, getting bigger and bigger, and then he'll take the blanket off my bodybox and lift the lid.

SMALL

I got lucky cause I'm small.

After that Syndicate soldier with the buzzpen put that Thirty-three on my arm, me and Shale was crying cause we was next to get sent down. They made us count off in twelves and Shale was Twelve and I was One which meant we wasn't going down to the Pits together and here comes Tick Burrowman with his bodybox and his hammer and nails, asking can he have someone from the line to show them how a kid could fit in the bodyboxes and he points to me and calls me over with his finger and I eat my crying and climb into the box and he nails down the lid and the world goes black, and I hear the Syndicate voices and Tick Burrowman's voice outside the bodybox like some bees buzzing and the next thing I know I feel like I'm floating in water and Tick Burrowman is carrying me up and away and he's talking to me through the wood all soft and gentle, going, *Don't worry, Thirty-three. Don't you worry now.*

He sang this little song that didn't have no words and that song kind of got inside the bodybox with me and made that blackness seem okay.

He didn't know I was Whensday Bluehouse from the Holy

Family Agency. All he knowed was that I'm little and that I'm a girl and that I got two different color eyes and red hair and that I would fit in the box without wiggling too much.

The next thing I know, the bodybox nails is getting yanked and the lid slides off and I'm inside Tick Burrowman's life hole, right on top of his planing table, and there's all these little candles burning and I'm crying cause all I can think about is Shale Bluehouse and how he's going down to the Pits and how that Thirty-two on his arm looks all sad and lonesome and how he'll wind up in one of them bodyboxes but how his bodybox won't get carried nowhere.

Tick Burrowman says the Syndicate needs the bodyboxes now cause they runned out of quickdust. The quickdust makes you disappear. Tick Burrowman says that after a Digit Kid croaks, this Syndicate soldier they call the Boxman comes around with this big honking box of white dust and sprinkles it over the body and then like two days later you don't even *see* the body no more, like that Digit Kid got erased with the end of a big *pencil* or something.

Tick Burrowman says the Digit Kids croak from busting rocks so hard and drinking the rain and eating sticks and mud and that after they croak they just lay down in the rockholes they spent all that time making with their splittingpicks.

When a Digit Kid makes their last lay the Syndicate soldiers don't want to touch them cause the croaked body is *toxic*. Even though he can't read, Tick Burrowman says toxic means *poi-*

sonous. He says that since they runned out of quickdust the Syndicate makes the other Digit Kids put the croaked bodies in the bodyboxes so they don't got to touch the bodies themselves.

Tick Burrowman says the Syndicate calls it *making your last lay* cause the word *croaking* sounds too sad. It's funny how a word can make something less sad than it really is.

Like the word *canister*.

Like the word *Syndicate*.

The word *birthpaper* is sad too cause it's like you ain't even alive unless you got one. This one Holy Family Agency nun called Sister Ricky Toots gave all of us Bluehouse kids our birthpapers right before the Syndicate came. Sister Ricky Toots had a big birthmark on her chin that looked like a food-blob and she didn't smell too good but she was always trying to help you. She teached me and Shale to read and make letters and stuff. Sister Ricky Toots told us Bluehouse kids to hide our birthpapers where no one would ever find them. She said that if you can prove you're twelve, the Syndicate can't clinch you no more cause you're old enough to be put to work. I turn twelve in like ten more minimonths. I ain't sure what I'm going to do after that. I ain't even sure if Tick Burrowman's going to be able to hide me for that long.

I got my birthpaper folded up real small and hided in my nest. For some reason, the Brownhouse and Greenhouse kids didn't never get their birthpapers. I even think some of the ones who is down in the Pits busting rocks *is* twelve. That ain't even right if you think about it.

The funny thing about my birthpaper is there's these two boxes that they're supposed to check to say whether you're a boy or a girl, but for some reason no one never checked mine. Both my boxes is empty like I ain't *nothing*. Like I'm a *rock* or a *stick*, not no *kid*.

VOICES

Hello, Mr. Burrowman.

Hidy, ma'am. Come in, come in. Get on out of that rain. Can I hang your coat?

I'll leave it on, thank you.

Sure, sure.

I can't stay.

I know, I know.

It's a long drive back.

Can't imagine.

You have no idea how long.

I reckon I don't. Care for some water?

I don't know that the water around here is fit to drink, Mr. Burrowman.

Oh, the water in my life hole's clean, ma'am. Clean as kittenpaws.

Kittenpaws, huh?

That's right. Scrubbed and boiled.

I'll take a glass, thank you.

There you go. No cobalt. No bugs. Just the clean clear tears of God. Sup it up now . . . How's that taste?

It tastes like water.

Good, good.

That rain is doing awful things to the paint on my automobile.

It's hellified, ma'am.

Mr. Blushing's going to have to repaint it every time I visit. Never knew a car to rust through the glovebox in its first three months.

Crazy rain is burnin the snot outta just about everything.

It'll give Mr. Blushing something to do during his down time.

I spose it will . . .

. . .

. . .

How is she, Mr. Burrowman?

She's fine.

Fine meaning?

Fine meanin fine.

I'd appreciate some details. I came all this way.

She's fine as a flower.

She's still . . .

Still what?

. . .Well, clean.

She's healthy as all get-out, ma'am. Healthier than healthy.

Pictures, Mr. Burrowman. Paint me *pictures*.

What can I tell you this time?

Her eyes. Tell me about her eyes.

Her eyes. Well, they're unusual.

Unusual?

Differnt.

Different?

That's right.

They use those words when they talk about slow children.

Well, them eyes of hers ain't slow, that's for sure.

Are they too close together?

I'd say they're spread just right.

She's walleyed?

No ma'am, not in the least.

One eye is permanently sealed.

It ain't that either.

She's bug-eyed.

No ma'am.

Her eyes leak strange fluids.

Never seen that before.

Unusual . . . Different . . . You make it sound as though she has some kind of de*form*ity, Mr. Burrowman.

Well, they're two different colors.

What colors?

One's blue, the other's green.

Green as in hazel?

Green as in green.

Green green?

That's correct.

Like gems or lawngrass?

Gems.

Emeralds?

An emyrald in the left.

And the right?

The right is blue.

Blue as in how blue?

Blue as an Easter egg. Blue as the bluest water. The cleanest coolest washed water there is.

Blue and green . . .

Green in the left, blue in the right.

That's yellow. Or amber!

They don't blend, ma'am. One's blue. The other's green. Just like socks or mittens.

Well, they sound lovely.

They *are* lovely, ma'am. They're lovely indeed.

And her skin. Tell me about her skin, Mr. Burrowman.

Pale as paper. Whiter than snow.

Any blemishes or birthmarks?

A freckle here and there. Nothin to be alarmed about.

No spots.

No ma'am. Like I said, she's healthier than healthy.

Do you examine her on a regular basis?

I see what I see. She don't got no hotspots.

Is she menstruating yet?

No ma'am. Not yet.

Perhaps she keeps it from you.

We don't keep nothin from each other.

Children can be tenacious with their secrets.

It ain't like that between us.

Really, Mr. Burrowman?

Really.

You're so sure.

I ain't so nothin, I just know her.

And her sleeping patterns?

Regular as a clockwatch.

She doesn't howl out in the night.

No ma'am.

She doesn't wander in her sleep.

If she do I ain't aware of it.

And her constitution?

She's strong as a thunderhorse.

Good structure?

Sturdy as a post.

No sudden dizzy spells, no vomiting?

Nothing like that. No ma'am. Food takes to her like sunshine to the spring. Like buds to a flower.

Oh, the *spring*, the *spring*.

That's right.

You all must miss the spring terribly here at the Shelf.

Miss it sorely, ma'am. Miss the daffydills. Miss them a lot.

I don't know how you all live in such conditions. I've never in my life smelled such foulness in the air.

That's them Pits.

The dreaded *Pits*. Even in Toptown we hear about the *Pits*.

Your nose forgets.

It forgets?

After a spell it don't even know them smells is there. Same way you forget about somethin bein in your pocket. Like a sticka gum or a pennycopper. How's that water?

It's fine, Mr. Burrowman. Not quite cold enough, but it's fine.

Care for some cheese?

God no.

You get hungry you just let me know.

What about her urine?

Golder than gold.

Nothing black. No discoloring?

She's as clean as a Christmas card, ma'am.

Kittenpaws and Christmas cards.

That's right.

I'd like to see her.

Well.

Well *what*, Mr. Burrowman?

That ain't part of the deal just yet.

Of course. A deal's a deal.

Now you *know* that, ma'am. We *talked* about all that.

But how am I to know she's *clean*? How am I to be *sure*?

You'll have to take my word for it.

Your word.

That's right. It's about the only thing I got left that God gave me.

THE BABYMAKERS
AND THE LOST MEN

The Babymakers got a life hole where the Lost Men go lay. Tick Burrowman says that the men who wasn't good enough for the Syndicate got sent down to the Pits before the Digit Kids. The ones who got away is called the Lost Men and they don't got nobody—no family and no women or nothing. They just roam the Shelf and hunt for food and plastic and fire and sleep in compost bins.

The compost bins is these big honking garbage dumps that got doors. The doors got numbers on them and during the doubleday the doors is left open so everyone from the Shelf can dump their garbage. But at night this Syndicate soldier called the Boltman locks them with these huge buckle latches. Tick Burrowman says the Boltman locks them so can't nobody sleep in them and so the Syndicate can protect the garbage so they can study it to see if there's anything *useful* they might want to keep.

Tacks and nails and old carparts is useful.

Shovel handles and hammerheads is useful, too.

Tick Burrowman says the Boltman has like a gazillion keys jangling on his belt and that he whistles this old church song and that you can hear him coming from a long ways off cause of the keys and also cause he whistles so good.

At night the Lost Men wait for the Boltman to make his sweep and after he's gone back down to the Pits they pick the buckle latches and sleep in the compost bins.

The Babymakers is lucky cause they don't got to live in no compost bins. They got a secret life hole and Tick Burrowman says when it opens you can see the light glowing right out of the rock. He says they got this big honking generator wheel hooked up to a electricity stove and that they got Christmas lights spiderwebbed over the walls and enough pots and pans to wash their water three times a doubleday. He says they take turns riding this bike that don't move so they can keep the generator wheel spinning. He says they call the bike the Dynamo Bike.

All the Babymakers care about is making babies cause they think Astan Loe is killing the world with people control. Most of the Babymakers is girls who was too old for the Pits and too young for the Flying Fox, but they was fast enough to run from the Black Bus, this old schoolbus that looks like someone drove it out of a volcano.

Tick Burrowman says after they lock you to this railing on the Black Bus the driver takes you to this doctor who cuts you open and steals all your babymaking parts.

Tick Burrowman says the driver don't tell those girls that they're busing them to the hospital to have their insides took out. Tick Burrowman says the driver tells them that they're going to the hospital for medicine so they don't get Blackfrost.

The Syndicate don't know about the Babymakers yet. Tick Burrowman says it's cause they're so quiet. They got a No Talking rule in their life hole. He says you can sit with them and lay with them and eat with them for hours and they don't never speak. He says they use these little chalkboards to talk and that all you hear when you're with them is the sound of the Dynamo Bike and the sound of chalk whispering on their chalkboards. The Babymakers hunt for Lost Men the same way the Lost Men hunt for food and plastic and fire.

Once this Babymaker came by to give Tick Burrowman a note. You could barely hear her but you could smell the rain burning her clothes.

I snucked out of my bodybox and looked through the slip curtain. She was wearing this long cloak. It had a hood and it was dark the way treeshade is dark and it looked like it would be soft if you touched it. You could see how the top of the hood was wet and how white her cheeks was and how her eyes was big and round and blue. And they wasn't blue the way no regular eyes is blue. They was blue the way a *song* is blue. I wanted to come out from the back but I didn't. I just stayed behind the slip curtain and stared at her.

After she left, Tick Burrowman came back and asked me to read the note to him cause he can't read. Sister Ricky Toots teached me and Shale how to read from this book called *Helicopters and Gingerbread*. That book was like a gazillion years old but the pictures had good colors and the letters was so big you could trace them with your finger.

The note went:

DEAR MR. BURROWMAN:
We request your services. Please come by our life hole at your earliest convenience.

Tick Burrowman went to the Babymakers' life hole like four times last minimonth but I think his dinker's croaked. They gave him this tube of special lotion that's supposed to uncroak his love muscles. Once he left it on the planing table and I took the tube and rubbed some into my arm. It was yellow and slippery and it smelled like dog pee. I put some on my privacy, too, cause I thought it might make my babymaking parts grow faster, but it didn't do nothing but make me feel like I sat down in the rain with no pants on.

The second time that Babymaker woman with the blue eyes came to visit Tick Burrowman, she handed him another note. It was about this one Lost Man called Inch Bluestroke.

Even though Inch Bluestroke is handsome and strong and Tick Burrowman says he would have made a good soldier, for some reason he hided from the Syndicate. Tick Burrowman says it's cause his wife croaked and that he got so sad that he wouldn't come out from this room that's under the floor of his life hole. Tick Burrowman says his wife's name was June and that she had red hair like me and that she had a chipped tooth but she was real pretty anyways. When Astan Loe and the Syndicate made their third people-counting sweep, they still couldn't find Inch Bluestroke under the floor of his life hole. Tick Burrowman says it's kind of a miracle cause of how the ditch dogs got those snufflebrains in their noses.

One doubleday when he needed to borrow some washed water, Tick Burrowman went over to Inch Bluestroke's life hole and while he was closing the door he heard this crash. When he opened the trapdoor he finded Inch Bluestroke laying on the floor with a rope tied around his neck. The rope had snapped where it was tied to a beam in the ceiling. Tick Burrowman says Inch Bluestroke hadn't ate in like a gazillion days and he was all skinny and ballistic-looking and his rib bones looked like big honking leg bones pressing through his skin. He says he was trying to *croak* himself with that rope.

Tick Burrowman hided Inch Bluestroke in his life hole for a bunch of minimonths and teached him how to clean trees and work the planing table. They became pretty good friends and when Inch Bluestroke stopped thinking those croaking thoughts Tick Burrowman let him back out to roam the Shelf and make his own way.

Inch Bluestroke used to sneak over to eat the Oldmonday mush. He had brown hair and brown eyes and you could always see the veins curling all blue and private in the tops of his hands.

Tick Burrowman says the Babymakers liked Inch Bluestroke cause he was so handsome. He had these big brown smoky eyes that made you feel like you had something warm in your stomach. I used to watch him through the slip curtain. I liked the way he walked all slow and careful, too, like he had something heavy in his shoes. He was by far the handsomest creature I've ever seen.

And Inch Bluestroke was sad, but it ain't like he was sad cause the *world* is sad. I would've married him and laid with him and maked his baby if I was old enough, but I ain't even twelve yet. My babymaking parts is *still* too small.

Inch Bluestroke was always talking about his wife and how her hair smelled like apples and how she played a metal flute and how she could whistle better than a man cause of that chip in her tooth and how they was planning on having a baby before the Creature Clouds came. His voice would go flat and tired and when he got like that it made me want to come out from the back and curl up in his lap so he could feel the muscles in my heart going ballistic next to his pocket.

So after that Babymaker with the blue eyes gave Tick Burrowman the note about Inch Bluestroke, she asked him when he was planning on coming over to help them make a baby. She didn't use no words, but you could tell what she was asking by the way she was making love pictures with her hands and fingers.

When I read the note about Inch Bluestroke to him, Tick

Burrowman had to sit down. And he didn't sit on no chair and he didn't sit on the planing table and he didn't sit on none of the trees that was cleaned and stacked. Tick Burrowman sat right on the *floor* and started snuffling into his hand. And he snuffled the way a little kid snuffles when he loses his kite or some marbles or something. That's when I started snuffling too. I started snuffling too cause the note said that one of the Babymakers finded Inch Bluestroke hanging from a branch of a Bone Tree.

JOE PAINTER
AND THE POT OF BEANS

One doubleday Tick Burrowman started marking off the rain days on the wall by the slop closet. He used this little piece of blue chalk and pressed so hard you could see the numbers all the way on the other side of the life hole. It was almost like those numbers started drawing themselves. It seemed like the numbers changed from Seventy to Eighty when you was sleeping.

Tick Burrowman didn't get no visitors for a long time. No Lost Men. No Babymakers. Even Second Staff Brown stopped coming up for his daily bodybox count.

Tick Burrowman thought that the Syndicate made more quickdust. I think he got nervous that they wouldn't need him to build no more bodyboxes cause he kept kind of twitching and wrestling with his lungpuddles and talking about the Flying Fox and how it used to be something people rode for fun.

But he just kept making the bodyboxes and drawing those numbers on the wall. Getting no visitors made those numbers seem bigger and bluer and heavier. Eighties felt like Nineties and Nineties felt like big honking Hundreds. The only way I can explain it is like this: if you could hold the number One in your hand it would probably feel more like you was holding a big heavy *stick* or a hunk of *Shelf rock*.

You could still hear the rain sliding and the Digit Kids busting rocks and you could sometimes even hear the hum from the fishflies. Things was pretty plain and gray.

Me and Tick Burrowman would do a self-clean every halfweek. They say Blackfrost bugs'll start crawling on you if you don't stay clean. When you get Blackfrost your pee turns black and then you go blind and hear all these churchbells in your head and then you curl up real small like a little baby and croak. There wasn't no such thing as Blackfrost before the Creature Clouds came.

You can tell who's got Blackfrost cause of the hotspots. The hotspots is these little purple marks you get all over your neck that itch and swell and ooze this boogery stuff. Some of the Undertwelves from the Numbering Line had the black smears on the front of their pants, too, and you could smell them and they didn't smell like no pee. They smelled more like something you find croaked under a *rock*.

Tick Burrowman would pull out this hunk of soap that smelled like apples and honey and we'd take turns standing in the metal tub and pass each other cooked water.

When he's naked, Tick Burrowman looks like a old crooked turkey who lost all his feathers. He's got this caved-in chest and his dinker's all bald and croaky-looking like this little plastic doll's arm that I finded under one of the beds at the Holy

Family Agency. Shale used to carry it around in his pocket and flick it with his thumb.

When Tick Burrowman would finish washing I'd hand him this old fireproof blanket and he'd wrap himself and walk over to his bed and fall asleep. Shale used to do stuff like that when we was at the Holy Family Agency. Every time he came out of the Bluehouse shower room he would fall dead asleep with this big dumb smile on his face.

During the doubleday Tick Burrowman started teaching me how to clean trees and help him at the planing table. He showed me how to use the hammer and scrape fishflies with the mattock stick.

The back room got so full of bodyboxes that you couldn't even pull the slip curtain all the way.

All those bodyboxes crammed in the back room made it hard for me to hide. The only two times I had to hide was when they came by to drop off the Oldmonday mush and when Joe Painter ducked through the front with Tick Burrowman's pot of beans.

Joe Painter's got a man's body but still seems like a boy cause of how big and scared-looking his eyes is. He's tall and his legs is all knotted up with muscles and when he talks his voice goes all low and sleepy. His mansmells is thick and kind of spicy and he's always sweaty from chopping and dragging and stacking trees for Tick Burrowman. He's always got this look on his face like he don't know why he's doing what he's doing, like he got *tricked* or something.

When he came ducking through the front of Tick Burrowman's life hole I didn't have time to get inside my bodybox so I had to sneak into the back.

You could hear Tick Burrowman saying hello and taking Joe Painter's greatcoat and offering him some of the washed water we cooked that morning.

When Joe Painter drinked the water you could hear his throat glurp and you could hear Tick Burrowman thanking him for chopping and dragging his trees in and you could hear him clearing his lungpuddles and thanking him again for bringing the pot of beans. And you could hear Joe Painter talking about how the Syndicate was still looking for the chicken broth and how he would have to come by in a few days to drop it off, and then you could hear Tick Burrowman going, No problem, no problem, Joe Painter, and then they was silent for a long time.

I thought that was all they was going to say to each other cause of how long they just sat there all quiet and dead-sounding. You could hear the groans from the Creature Clouds. It was like they was hungry.

Then Tick Burrowman asked him about how things was going and what it was like working in the rain and if the hatchetaxe that the Syndicate gave him was sharp enough and Joe Painter answered him all simple and kind of quiet with *Okays* and *Uh-huhs* and stuff like that.

Then you could hear Tick Burrowman fiddling in the sinkwell and then, for some reason, Joe Painter started *crying* and it was like his crying was the wind whistling through the cracks. It sounded more like a little *kid's* crying than the crying of someone who had a deep voice and mansmells and muscle-knots in his legs.

You could hear Tick Burrowman patting him on the back and going, It's okay, young fella, it's okay, everything's gonna be fine, don't you worry, and I couldn't figure out what was going on cause there wasn't enough words mixing with the crying.

Tick Burrowman was like, You go head and let it out. Let it right out, Joe Painter. You go right on head now, young fella, and then Joe Painter would kind of huff and catch his breath and start crying again.

After Joe Painter drinked some more and settled down, his voice went all high and wobbly and he started talking about how he had to go down to the Pits to take some new boots to one of the Syndicate soldiers. He talked about how he climbed down the rock ladder with the new boots slinged over his shoulder and how the rock ladder was all slick from the rain and how he met the First Staff who ordered the new boots and how the First Staff took off his rotten boots right there and put on the new ones and set the rotten ones on fire. And Joe Painter talked about the smell of the old boots and the smell of the tires burning and how he could still taste it in his nose and he talked about all the fishflies and how they was flying in big sheets and how the fishfly sheets was falling and dipping cause of the smoke from the burning tires and he talked about the sound of the splittingpicks and how they kept clank-clank-clanking and how he stopped hearing the clanking after a minute cause there was so much of it.

Then Joe Painter talked about how all of the Syndicate soldiers was walking around with guns and electricity sticks and canteens of washed water but how none of the Digit Kids had washed water and how they looked so lost and tired and how some of them couldn't even raise their splittingpicks over their heads. And Joe Painter said how some of the Syndicate soldiers was poking the Digit Kids cause they wasn't busting rocks fast enough and how some of them had bloodspots on their backs.

Tick Burrowman gave him some more washed water from the sinkwell and patted him on the back and you could hear Joe Painter's throat glurping again, and after he finished the water Joe Painter talked about this little boy who he seen laying in a bodybox and how his arm was all flopped out like there wasn't no bones in it and how one of the Syndicate soldiers asked him to push that arm in the box so they could nail the lid down and how he did it and how the little boy's eyes was all rolled back and how his mouth was open like he wanted food.

He said all that to Tick Burrowman and Tick Burrowman just kept going, *Sh-sh, sh-sh, sh-sh, it's okay, Joe Painter, it's okay, son.*

Then Joe Painter started crying again and it sounded like he was crying into his hand or the side of his arm maybe, and I kept picturing that little boy in the bodybox and how Joe Painter had to push that arm over the side and how they nailed the lid down and I could hear those nails getting popped with a hammer and I could hear the popping of the nails mixing with the clanking of the splittingpicks and the burning of the tires and the humming of the fishflies, and I could picture that bodybox getting stacked on top of a bunch of other ones and how it might be like a big lost *wall* and I could picture how sad and lonesome that bodybox wall looked, and then for some reason I kept seeing *Shale* and I could see his face and his eyes and his mouth and I started thinking about how he used to call me Wendy at first, how he couldn't say Whensday cause some of his teeth was missing, and how he always slept with his mouth a little open cause he couldn't breathe through his nose cause he was allergic to powdered milk, and I kept picturing how you could see the little spaces from where Shale Bluehouse's new teeth was supposed to be coming in, and how he liked to call them his new choppers, and then I didn't even realize it, but I was walking through the stacks of bodyboxes and through the slip curtain and down the hallway and my walking was like the kind of walking you do in a dream when there's voices behind a door and you're walking toward those voices, and then I was standing right in front of the planing table where they was sitting and I took Joe Painter's hand and he looked at me and went down to his knees and he quit crying and his face went real still and he just stared at me and you could barely hear the breath slipping in and out of his lungbags.

For some reason Tick Burrowman didn't mind. It was the first time I ever done that and it was dangerous cause of Joe Painter being with the Syndicate and me being a Undertwelve and having the Thirty-three on my arm and all, but it was too late to go back.

Joe Painter took both of my hands and held them in front of his face and then he covered his eyes and nose and mouth with them and I could feel his hot breath on my fingers and I could smell his mansmells coming thick and peppery.

Tick Burrowman just sat there all lopsided and crooked-looking like he wasn't sure what to do.

Joe Painter cried into my hands for a long time and he cried the way a boy cries.

After a while he stopped and Tick Burrowman gave him some more washed water and helped him off the floor and thanked him for the pot of beans.

Joe Painter looked at me and then turnt to Tick Burrowman and they nodded and their nodding was private and then Joe Painter ducked back through the front of Tick Burrowman's life hole and out into the sliding rain.

VOICES

Hello again, Mr. Burrowman.

Evenin, ma'am.

Don't touch my coat.

Sorry.

This coat is of no concern to you.

I spose it ain't.

No concern at all.

You okay, ma'am?

Of course I'm okay.

You look a bit flussied.

Well, I'm starting to find this place incredibly depressing.

Well . . .

Well *what*? You're always saying *Well*.

. . . Well . . .

There are plenty of words to describe what's going on out there. *Well* just doesn't seem to do it for me.

Times have been tricky for a while now.

My driver calls it Shelf Life.

Mr. Blushing.

That's right. Mr. Blushing. People in Toptown call it Babylon.

Around here we call it livin.

Living like rats and vermin.

Livin's livin, no matter how you slice it.

There's no hope here.

Well, there ain't no rats here, neither. Not no more.

The Creature Clouds this. The Blackfrost that. Fishflies and sodabushes. What in Job's name is a fishfly anyway?

Once them prevailin winds come, things'll get back to what they was. You just got to be patient.

Sometimes patience turns into years, Mr. Burrowman. And years into lives. In this case, lost lives.

I reckon you're right.

Let's get on with it then.

Care for some water?

No. I don't care for your water and I don't care for your blocks of cheese.

So how can I help you this evenin?

I want to know her name.

That ain't part of the deal, ma'am.

I want to know her damn name. Tell it to me.

That comes later.

How much later?

Later when things is finalized later.

We've already talked about terms, Mr. Burrowman.

But you ain't shown me nothin yet.

I don't just start handing things over without knowing

what I'm getting.

Then I guess I don't got no name for you.

Suppose I were to give you a small amount right now. To show my good faith.

How small is small?

Five hundred halfknots.

On top of the agreed amount?

On top of the agreed amount.

You put that kinda money in my hand and I might just come up with a name for you.

It's in my right pocket. In a brown paper sack.

There?

Yes, there.

Woo-*wee*.

Spare me the cheerleading, Mr. Burrowman.

Lot heavier than it looks.

There's no need to count it.

Oh, I'm gonna count it, ma'am, don't you worry. I'm gonna count every note right as the rain is gray.

Well, count away.

Tin, twinny, thirty, forty . . .

You have no idea what it is to crave a child, do you, Mr. Burrowman?

Can't say that I do.

The ache. The boredom.

I know what it is to care for one. Ninety, a hunnert, hunnertin. To tend to it as if it was my own.

You count and I'll talk.

I'm with you, ma'am. I'm right here with you.

The body fails us in the end, Mr. Burrowman. I'm sure you know that as well as I. It betrays us. The womb shrivels up. Voids itself like some lost pocket on the Moon. You can feel the emptiness. The wind blowing through you. I knew that feeling was coming long before it arrived. It's as though God himself hides his hand inside you. His long, invisible hand. And then the years start adding up. The body starts slipping away. Your breasts sag. Your flesh loosens and turns to rubber. The light fades in your eyes. And the womb disappears. It's yanked and plucked and gorged. And what is left is indescribable. An indescribable thing, Mr. Burrowman. You take lovers. You buy them like curtains. You change the wallpaper. You focus on other things. But the void is always there. The gaping void. You'll never know that feeling, Mr. Burrowman.

I spose I won't, ma'am.

You cough entirely too much.

It's a nervous habit.

Do I make you nervous?

You're just a little noisy is all.

You count money like a gasoline attendant.

Never tended a pump in my life.

You have interesting hands.

Carpentry'll do funny things to em.

The hands of a battered man.

Battered but still standin. Still standin and still countin . . . If my math is correct there's five hundred solid here.

Are you satisfied?

Like a fox in a henhouse.

I want her name.

And I'm gonna tell it to you, ma'am. But I got one question first.

I'm not paying you to ask questions.

Well, grant me one out of everlovin goodness then.

What is it, Mr. Burrowman?

Why you want her name so bad? It don't matter, do it?

I'm having things monogrammed. Sweaters. Scarves. Bobbysocks. It's something I like to do. I imagine her. Her black hair. Her blue eye. Her green eye. Her pale skin.

Her hair's red, ma'am.

Then I'll start imagining it red.

Red as a haybarn and curly as a sodabush.

I imagine that and I want to name the things she will have. I want to have them thoroughly sewn and stitched. I want her to walk into a room and know how firmly she belongs.

Her name is Thirty-three.

Thirty-three.

That's right. That's what I call her. That's what she answers to.

They go by numbers now?

I'm afraid so, ma'am.

For the love of Job.

Your hands is shakin.

Thirty-three, of all things! *Dogs* get better names!

You sure you wouldn't care for some water?

I don't want your filthy water!

THE OFFERTORY

In the ninety-third doubleday of rain, Slocumb Yardly comes running through the Shelf shouting through his bullhorn. He's going ballistic about how Astan Loe's on his way with the collection wagon. When he runs, Slocumb Yardly's feet sound like twenty men's feet. Can't nobody in the Syndicate clinch him.

You can hear Slocumb Yardly knocking on the front of life holes and yelling through his bullhorn, going *Astan Loe, Astan Loe!* and you can hear Astan Loe's big black thunderhorse clopping all the way on the other side of the Shelf and those clops is so loud it's like God made them special that way. And behind the clopping of Astan Loe's thunderhorse you can hear the creaking of the collection wagon and the wheels turning and going *skreet-skreet-skreet*, and you can hear all the Syndicate soldiers knocking on doors and collecting with their Offertory buckets.

I don't recognize the Syndicate man's voice, but I can hear his boots stomping and the tail of his greatcoat swooshing over the floor.

I know it ain't Second Staff Brown and I know it ain't Joe Painter and I know it ain't the Syndicate man who brings the

Oldmonday mush cause it ain't Oldmonday.

The Syndicate man asks if Tick Burrowman's got aluminum and Tick Burrowman's like, Yessir. One pretty fair ball of aluminum comin right up.

Through the hole I can see Tick Burrowman holding the aluminum ball. The candleflames from the hallway dance off it so it looks like he's holding a little lost star.

The Syndicate soldier takes the aluminum ball and drops it into the Offertory bucket like he's dropping it into a *toilet*.

It's funny how a Syndicate soldier can do what he wants just cause of the way his greatcoat swooshes and the way his boots stomp and the way the light flashes fancy off those silver snaps on his pants. It don't matter to him that it was like a little silver planet and that I used to think about being on it while it was spinning away through space, and how maybe Shale Bluehouse would be on it with me and how we would be waving back down to the world, going *Bye-bye, you big dumb lost world!* and stuff like that.

You can hear them opening and closing the front of the life hole and you can hear Tick Burrowman pushing and grunting and cursing the Creature Clouds. I picture Tick Burrowman holding his leg and kind of leaning sideways and catching his breath.

You think that that Syndicate soldier might *talk* to Tick Burrowman but he don't. You think he might say *Thanks, Tickyman* or *Good night, Tick* or *Take it slow, Tickytack* or something, but all you hear is his big black boots stomping away.

I think Syndicate soldiers get their voices took away. It's easier to make people do stuff when they can't scream or cry or laugh. I think that's how come you can get a ditch dog to do things like fetch and run and chase Undertwelves. They don't got no voices, so it's like they got to do what another voice says.

Maybe that Syndicate doctor who steals babymaking parts can take voices, too.

VOICES

And her parents?

Don't know much.

They're not dead?

Couldn't tell you.

Don't you think that's some information I might want to be *privy* to?

I imagine so.

It's rather pertinent, I'd say, Mr. Burrowman.

I can only tell you what I know, ma'am.

I wouldn't want a strange woman showing up on my doorstep. A poor woman in rags. Some Shelf leech in a *shawl* with *hotspots* all over her arms.

I doubt that'll happen, ma'am.

But you can't be *sure*, Mr. Burrowman? People have a funny way of reclaiming what was once theirs. A funny, funny way. Don't you agree?

I spose, ma'am. I spose.

You know nothing of a mother. A father.

Wasn't in the book.

Oh, this *book*, this *book*. I'd like to see this *book*.

I'm sure Mosely'd show it to you if you asked.

I don't trust books. Never did.

Well, it's the only thing we got to go on. Mosely swears by it.

And what the hell is in this book?

It's all the registered children under twelve. Indexed and digested. Every last one of em. From before the Creature Clouds right up to now. Mosely showed it to me, ma'am.

I suppose our little friend has her own page.

She's in there.

I can just see it. Her hair done up in curls. Her teeth gleaming like the Sun.

Oh, they don't put their pitchers in the book. But she's in there, ma'am. She's in there right as the rain is gray. Didn't say nothin about no parents. Mosely says all them Holy Family kids is orphans. They got three big houses full. A blue house, a brown house, and a green house.

And Minister Minifield can be trusted with these matters?

Course he can. Man of the Lord. Man of good intentions. I'd lay down my life for that man.

And he for you?

If I was worthy.

And are you worthy?

I'd like to think so, ma'am.

You get a funny look on your face when you're proud, Mr. Burrowman.

Everyone gets a look or two.

A streak of pink across your cheek. A telling flush.

Never was much of a poker player.

A funny little look for a funny little man.

I spose you came all this way again just to tell me how funny and little I am.

If that was the case this would be a sadder world than it already is.

So what is we talkin about me for?

Tell me where she came from.

Like I told you, them folks at the Holy Family Agency found her in a compost bin.

Right. With the fishheads and rotten eggs.

Found her folded in the newspaper.

Another baby wrapped in headlines. Yesterday's news.

That's where she came from.

And she just found her way to you. Like a stray cat in the alleyway.

It wasn't no accident.

You think God had something to do with it.

Well . . .

You think it was divine inter*vention*.

All I'm sayin is it was awfully uncanny the way she wound up in my bodybox.

Uncanny as in . . .

Well, let me put it thisaway.

You put it, Mr. Burrowman.

When I was lookin at that line of Digit Kids, the whole

line of em . . .

Go on.

Now you prolly ain't gonna believe what I'm about to say, ma'am.

Just get on with it, Mr. Burrowman. Please.

Well, when I was lookin at that line of Undertwelves somethin awful peculiar happened . . .

Which was?

Well, she was the only one I was seein.

I don't follow you.

You see, I knew all them other little ones was there. Like I could *hear* em. I could *feel* em standin there. Hell, I could even *smell* em cause of the way they was making accidents in their pants.

And?

Well, even though I knew they was there, she was the only one. It was like everyone else in that line disappeared. Like seein a golden hen in a field fulla black sheep.

One of God's wee and lovely spells.

There musta been twinny, thirty of them little ones lined up. Buzznumbered and ready to be sent down to the Pits. But she was the only one there. I called her out of the line and she crawled right into the bodybox.

So it was love at first sight.

Well . . .

Or we could call it love at first *crawl*.

I ain't too sure if any love was involved, ma'am. But whatever it was was a awful strong feelin. Awful strong.

I suppose you heard harps and Hail Marys.

No, ma'am. Didn't hear none of that.

But you felt it.

That I did, ma'am. Felt it right here in my chestbone. Like a tiny little bird flutterin.

When I feel tiny little birds fluttering in my chest it's usually indigestion.

You sure know how to put things, ma'am.

Go on.

Well, when we was finished, them Syndicate fellas didn't even remember she was still in the bodybox.

They didn't?

They just went about their business like she was back in line and ready to be sent down.

So you think she's a witch.

No ma'am. She ain't nothin of the sort.

A little *sorceress*.

I think she's special, ma'am. Special. That's what I think. *Special.*

Like there's a reason for her bein here.

TOPTOWN DREAMS

I dream about Toptown.

Sometimes the dream stays in me after I wake up, the same way the sound of the wind stays in your ear if you stand next to a crack in the wall too long.

I dream about swimming across the Red River. I dream about how the fishes start living again when you get close to the other side. Bluefishes and yellowfishes and redfishes. All those colors swimming under me and tickling my knees and my privacy.

I dream of sleeping on the banks of the other side. When I dreamsleep I dreamdream of the light busting through the sky where the Creature Clouds stop. Busting through like a big yellow river falling. And the way the trees grow and how they kind of whisper to each other through their leaves and the way a bird looks when it's flying real high, how it's all still and small, how it looks like something that got imagined by the Sun.

Then in my dream I wake up and look back across the water where the Bone Trees twist funny and kind of disappear into the sky.

I dream about the Forsaken Lawn.

I dream about how many days it would take to get to where

the Creature Clouds stop and the Sun starts shining regular again.

I dream about eating a orange, the same way me and Shale Bluehouse used to share a orange when there was still oranges to share. We would take turns peeling and break it up into sections and deal them like cards.

Whenever I dream about getting to Toptown I see this pretty lady with little blue flowers in her dress and she's got real pretty eyes and they're green the way my one eye is green and she smells nice and it's like the little blue flowers in her dress is making her smell nice. And she's got a smile that makes you feel like you got a little bird flying around inside you.

And next to her is this man who looks like Inch Bluestroke. He's got a handsome happysad face and his mansmells is clean like apples soaking in washed water and he's got blue eyes and they're blue the way my other eye is blue. And that man and that woman is standing together and they might even be holding hands or kind of leaning real nice against each other and then they call me. They go, *Come here, Whensday. Come here, daughter. It's time to go home.*

TICK BURROWMAN'S
CROOKED CANDLE

Last night I waked up and Tick Burrowman was standing over me. He was standing over me and with one hand he was holding his side and with his other hand he was holding this old crooked candle he uses when he gets up in the middle of the night to use the slop closet.

His lungbags was dragging air real slow, the same way thunder moves all slow and sleepy through the Creature Clouds. His eyes was all big and spooky-looking and his mouth was open like some food fell out.

I kept my eyes closed but I could still see him cause I was peeking through my lidslits.

He was wearing these funny old striped pajamas and his crooked candle was sawing and the flame was making his face look old and sad.

I thought he was going to come and sit on my halfbed, but he just stood there staring. He kept going, *Thirty-three, oh, Thirty-three*, and it was real quiet and lonesome-sounding.

You could hear the rain sliding up against the front of the life hole and you could hear the wind swooshing and there was this one little leak from a crack in the corner and it looked like God was drawing a line on the wall. I tried to watch that water line and not-watch Tick Burrowman's sad old face.

After a while he sat on the floor and set the crooked candle in front of him. Then he held his face in his hands and started making these little wheezing noises. I couldn't tell if he was crying or if he was just tired. He stayed there like that for a long time. I kept watching that water line through my lidslits.

Then for some reason Tick Burrowman started going, *My little girl, my poor little girl*, and *My little friend, my little friendly friend*, and stuff like that. He probably had a bad dream about me or something.

Sometimes I have this dream about Shale Bluehouse. He's walking through the Bone Trees and he's picking up penny-coppers and kind of whistling this song and then he falls and when I catch up to him he ain't there no more and then I look down and there's this big honking *black hole* and there ain't no bottom and all you can see is one of his *shoes* and it's all muddy and sad. The weird part is that when I really look I realize that it's one of *my* shoes that I let Shale have cause his got this big crack in the bottom and he had to wrap it with electricity tape so his foot wouldn't get wet. When I wake up I always got all these feelings of loneliness and the muscles in my heart ache. I ain't never told Shale how we was like brother and sister. I ain't never told him how I liked how he slept with his mouth open just enough so you could see how he was missing his two front teeth. I ain't never told him *none* of that stuff.

For some reason I think that's what was going on with Tick

Burrowman. He probably had one of them dreams and it was *me* who disappeared or got clinched or fell into the Pits or something.

He stayed on the floor like that for a long time. The crooked candle was in front of him and it was throwing funny shadows on the walls and those shadows was making everything feel strange.

I froze myself and tried to disappear in my halfbed.

I didn't open my eyes till he left.

MOSELY MINIFIELD

osely Minifield is Tick Burrowman's best friend. Tick Burrowman calls him Minny Moe and Mosely Minifield calls Tick Burrowman Tick-tack-toe.

Minny Moe!

Tick-tack-toe!

How's she go, Minny Moe?

Too fast for slow, Tick-tack-toe. Too fast for slow.

They laugh and hug and pat shoulders every time Mosely Minifield visits, like it's been a gazillion years since they seen each other.

Before the Creature Clouds came Mosely Minifield was a priest. Priest is a funny word cause there ain't no such thing as no priest no more. He had a church on the other end of the Shelf called the St. Lewis Arch of Jesus. It had this little bell-tower that looked like something a giant would hide his money in. On Oldsundays, Mosely Minifield would climb up to the top of the belltower and ring the evening vapors. The St. Lewis Arch of Jesus don't exist no more cause Astan Loe and his Syndicate men knocked it down with a hammerball.

Tick Burrowman says that one doubleday Astan Loe asked all the priests to give up their holycloaks and the ones who didn't was shot and the ones who did was took away in the Flying Fox.

Mosely Minifield's lucky cause he didn't get shot or took away like all the other Elders. Tick Burrowman says they didn't take Mosely Minifield away cause of Vern Soper. Vern Soper's the Syndicate man who operates the Flying Fox. Tick Burrowman says that even though religion ain't supposed to mean nothing no more, Vern Soper still believes in God, and he pulled Mosely Minifield off the line and helped him find a life hole in the Bone Trees so he could still take communion and get rid of his sins and stuff.

So when Mosely Minifield came ducking through Tick Burrowman's life hole, I thought he was going to start talking about God or give us some holy breadcircles to eat, but he didn't.

Mosely Minifield has a hard time keeping his hands still and even in the back I could see them shaking.

Tick Burrowman was like, What is it, Mosely? What is it? and then Mosely Minifield grabbed at his hands and told Tick Burrowman how someone stole all the aluminum foil out of Astan Loe's collection wagon. Mosely Minifield said he heard from Vern Soper how Astan Loe was coming back to the Shelf to hunt the thief. His voice was all nervous and wavery.

For some reason, that made me think of Mosely Minifield and how scared he must have been when he had to give up his holycloak. That made me think of how his hands is always going ballistic, and how even though he's supposed to be one of God's friends God ain't really done *nothing* for him.

EYES OF A THUNDERHORSE

I still don't know nothing about her except that you can smell her the way you could smell flowers when there was still flowers to smell. She ain't no Babymaker and she ain't no Sister from the Holy Family Agency and she ain't from the Syndicate cause there ain't no ladies in the Syndicate.

She wears this fancy perfume and gold earrings that is so big they look like these old trumpet horns me and Shale Bluehouse finded in the basement of the Holy Family Agency. Her face is all made up like a clown's face and when she speaks her voice sounds all clean and cold and perfect, like the kind of voice you used to hear on the radio when there was still voices on the radio.

I think she's from Toptown cause she drives to the Shelf in a long black car that looks like something you could live in. I seen it when I was washing water. Tick Burrowman was in the slop closet doing his business when I heard the motor. That motor sounded like a *rocket* or a *plane*.

I left the pot of washed water in the sinkwell, pulled the plastic bag over my head, and slipped through the front. The rain was going sideways and the wind was blowing through the Bone Trees and you could hear rocks getting busted in the Pits.

That car had mirrors on the windows and gloss on the wheels and the metal on the front was so shiny it looked like something you'd find in a *treasure* chest.

The motor purred and slowed and then that big long car door opened and I runned back inside and crawled into my bodybox so fast I forgot to take off Tick Burrowman's plastic bag.

She knocked on the front of the life hole like it was a little song she made up. Then you could hear Tick Burrowman finishing his business in the slop closet and going, Just a minute, and stuff, and then the slop closet opened and closed and Tick Burrowman coughed and spit and kind of hobbled through the kitchencove to the front.

I watched them through the hole. I had to be more still than ever cause of the way the plastic bag crumples.

At first I thought she might be Tick Burrowman's sister, but that didn't make no sense cause of her fancy coat and her fancy voice and her fancy makeup. When Tick Burrowman offered her some washed water, she said, No thank you, and started smoking this long brown cigarette that smelled like pepper and old leaves.

They wasn't saying my name, but I could tell they was talking about me cause of the way they kept going *She* and *Her*. Every time they said it it made me feel smaller and smaller. And those small feelings started making me tired. After like ten minutes I fell asleep.

I dreamed of a silver slit in the Creature Clouds. I was running to it the way people run for money when it's tumbling through the sky, but for some reason my running wasn't leading me nowhere. Then that silver slit started going smaller and smaller till it was swallowed by those big black bellies in the Creature Clouds.

When I waked up their voices was all sleepy and there was this long silence that was full of the sound of people scrambling on the Shelf and the sound of rain running on the door and the sound of thunder groaning all lost and hungry in the Creature Clouds.

They was still using *Shes* and *Hers* and *Yes she ises* and *No she's nots* and *No she ain'ts* and sometimes those *Shes* and *Hers* sounded like they was going ugly.

For some reason I was holding on to my bird's nest real hard. It felt like I would disappear if I let go.

So what will it be, Mr. Burrowman?

Tick Burrowman tapped his foot for a minute and said, Well, I gotta think on it some more.

It seems like that's all I come here for. To listen to you speak about your need to think.

Well, this is a tricky situation, ma'am. A tricky, hellified situation.

Too much thought killed the genius in his sleep.

I don't know what that meant and I don't think Tick

Burrowman did neither cause he just kept tapping his foot and the rain kept sliding and the thunder kept groaning in the Creature Clouds.

Then the old lady was like, We've been through it several times. I assure you that the best care will be taken.

I know, I know, Tick Burrowman said.

She'll get the best schooling. She'll have nice clothes. Clean water. A big room of her own.

Tick Burrowman was like, It's just that I've growed attached, and he said that part all quiet and lonesome.

I understand that, Mr. Burrowman, and I find that very moving.

It's a heckuva spot to be in.

I started petting my bird's nest like it was a mouse or a puppy.

I knowed one of those voices was Tick Burrowman's, but I didn't want to believe it. When I pictured him sitting there at the planing table with that lady, I kept not-seeing his face. I would see his skinny crooked goat legs and his old wrinkled hands and how they was all twisted up and spoily-looking, and I could even hear his tired old clutchingcough, but for some reason when I tried to picture his face I couldn't remember it.

The lady went, I'd like to think that twenty thousand half-knots is more than enough compensation.

Well . . .

I'd be willing to up it to thirty.

That's a mighty big offer, ma'am. Mighty big.

Mighty big indeed, Mr. Burrowman. You could do a lot with that kind of money.

You shore could, ma'am. You shore could.

Get away from the Shelf. Start over.

Start over . . .

Thirty-five thousand halfknots.

I could open up a shop, maybe. Get a little bandsaw. Some new tools.

You could probably get to Toptown with that kind of money, Mr. Burrowman.

. . . She's just so young yet, is all.

Mr. Burrowman, with the new laws, not many children have the opportunity for the kind of life I can offer. You have to think of what's *good* for her. You *must*.

Then they didn't say nothing for a minute and you could hear her lighting another cigarette. I just kept squeezing my bird's nest.

Does she like horses, Mr. Burrowman?

I couldn't say for sure. I think she could like just about anything.

I own a stable full of the finest thunderhorses around. Chargermounts. Quarterbucks. Perhaps she could learn to ride.

We don't think too highly of them thunderhorses around here, ma'am. With the Syndicate raisin em up from foals and all.

Well, that will be for her to decide.

It's a lot to think about.

I realize that. So think.

I will, ma'am. I'll do that.

I'd like very much to meet her.

In due time, ma'am. In due time.

I want to finish this business tomorrow. Mr. Blushing will drive me over to Minister Minifield's. That's where I will be. You'll bring her there in the morning. Eleven o'clock. I want her well-rested and sanitized. Is that clear? . . . Mr. Burrowman?

Yes ma'am.

Is that clear?

Clear as water, ma'am. Clear as water.

Good.

I didn't hear nothing after that cause there was thunder-screams in my head. I kept trying to not-picture her long dark car and not-picture Tick Burrowman's foot and how it was still tapping under the planing table.

I kept squeezing my nest till it hurted my hand.

II

HONEYCUT AND THE FISHFLIES

I waited till the middle of the night.

I felt smaller than ever. Smaller than a mouse or a frog. Smaller than a fishfly.

There was a big blue Ninety on the wall. It seemed like that Ninety just *appeared* there, like the *wall* drawed it blue or something.

I safe-jammed my arms and cheeks and took some cheese from the cupboard in the kitchencove and tucked it in my pants and headed toward the front of the life hole with the garbage bag pulled tight.

You could hear Tick Burrowman wrestling with his clutchingcough. It sounded like his lungpuddles was filling with rain. I went into his room and stood over him and watched his face twist and skitter like he was fighting someone in a dream.

You'd figure that the Syndicate would give Tick Burrowman some medicine for his lungpuddles. You'd figure that Second Staff Brown might come ducking through the life hole with a packet of *pep pills* or something, but he don't. To Second Staff Brown it's like Tick Burrowman's clutchingcough is part of everything else, like it's some rain or wind or a little black spot in the Creature Clouds.

I wanted to put my hand on Tick Burrowman's chest to smooth his breathing, but I couldn't. I thought if I did he might wake up and make a funny face or ask me to help him at the planing table. Then I would have froze. I would have froze like a little dumb snowman.

So I waited till Tick Burrowman started breathing regular again.

And then I left.

The Creature Clouds was like a bunch of old ditch dogs sleeping in the sky. When you looked up it made everything go real quiet in your head cause it seemed like they could just dive down and start chasing you.

The rain was sideways and you had to look at your shoes when you walked so it wouldn't get in your eyes. All you could see was steam rising out of the rock and the little bubbles popping and the rain sliding through the steam. It was so hot it felt like the ground was cooking.

In the Bone Trees you could see the steam curling through the naked branches. The rain was sliding through steam like it was something that was always there, like the wind or the sky or the caves in the Moon.

In the distance you could hear the ditch dogs growling through their muzzlestraps.

The Red River's at the bottom of the Bone Trees and I like to sneak down to the banks so I can watch this one fish that ain't been killed yet. My fish is white and when it swims it's like a big floppy hand flipping through the water. Most of the other fishes is dead cause they got boiled by the poison in the rain. Sometimes you'll see one washed up in the mud all brown and stiff like some wood. They call the ones that ain't died yet voodoo fishes, cause if you eat them they'll make your insides fall out. But my whitefish ain't no voodoo fish. My whitefish's got big crazy frog eyes and sometimes when I watch it swim it feels like it's talking to me.

When the fishflies jump, the water boils up and sprays all crazy like a big riverburp. They only live for a halfweek and as soon as they land they just cling to whatever they cling to till they croak. When me and Shale Bluehouse was in the Numbering Line all you heard was crunching cause of all the dead fishflies getting stepped on. I won't never forget that sound. It was like a bunch of old *dog bones* getting crushed.

I was hiding behind a sodabush when the fishflies started jumping. The sodabushes is the only plants around the Shelf that ain't been burnt by the rain. Sometimes if the compost bins is full, you'll see a Lost Man sleeping in one. You'll see his shoes or maybe some old newspapers pulled over them so the rain won't burn through the laces. The sodabushes is white and they get real snarly at the top and they smell cause of all the dooks that get left in them.

There's this one Lost Man called the Salt Man who just goes from compost bin to compost bin. He's a Elder and he's got this long greasy white beard. They say he's the best at picking the buckle latches and that the Syndicate ain't never going to clinch him. That's who I was watching down by the Red River after I left Tick Burrowman's life hole. The Salt Man was walking through the water and trying to not-fall. You could hear the wings of the fishflies beating and this little hum they make. Some people think that the Salt Man's got Blackfrost cause he's got so many hotspots and cause his pants is all blacksmeared in the front. But the Salt Man just keeps on living like Blackfrost can't touch him or something.

At first I thought he was trying to catch my whitefish. I was about to throw a rock at him but he started waving his arms and trying to catch the fishflies with his dumbhat. They call it his dumbhat cause it's so old and collapsed that it makes him look like he lost his mind inside of it.

The Salt Man used to come begging at the life hole. Tick Burrowman would cut him a corner of cheese, but he stopped after a while cause he said it was killing our supply. Now the Salt Man just wanders around the Shelf talking to his dumbhat and begging for food and plastic.

Tick Burrowman says the Salt Man's been wearing his dumbhat for thirty years and that he sleeps on it, eats out of it, and even prays into it. Tick Burrowman says if the Syndicate took his dumbhat away he would probably curl up like a little kid and croak cause his heart would break so hard.

You could hear him splashing in the water and cursing the

fishflies. After he finally catched some he lit them on fire with some matches and watched the fishflies burn right in the bowl of his hat. He was careful to blow out the flames so his dumbhat wouldn't catch fire. His eyes was so big it was like he was watching something that walks toward you in a dream.

For some reason he started shouting, *Four thousand fishflies! Four thousand fishflies!* and he was shouting it the way people shout when they think they see a silver slit burning in the Creature Clouds.

The Salt Man blew out the fire and it started smoking and then he *ate* the cooked fishflies. He ate the fishflies and his teeth turnt black the same way a house turns black after a fire.

He's lucky the Syndicate wasn't down there with their flamethrowers. They would have probably pointed them right at him and fried him the way they used to fry chickens and pigs when there was still chickens and pigs to fry. They would have probably looked away all bored and flatfaced when they did it, too.

After the Salt Man sucked the black off his teeth he put on his dumbhat and walked along the edge of the Red River and disappeared into the mist, and his disappearing was like a bag blowing away in the wind.

That's when I seen the giant.

He was sitting in the shallow end of the water and he was crying and his crying sounded like a ditch dog groaning for scraps. It didn't look right cause of how big he was. The fishflies was swelling up all around him and the water was boiling fast. At first I thought he was a Syndicate soldier who flipped his head.

He was sitting right in the water and he was crying through his nose and wiping his face and I know the poison in the water was making his eyes burn cause they was going ballistic and blinking like a blink festival. He wasn't wearing no garbage bag and he wasn't wearing no hat and he wasn't smeared with no safe jam, neither. You can tell when someone's smeared with the safe jam cause they look sticky.

The giant followed the last few fishflies with his big blobfinger and then he turnt and looked down at the water. He looked at the water for a long time and he was looking at it like he lost something that he wasn't never going to find again.

I was like, Whatcha lookin for?

He didn't say nothing. He kind of looked up and snuffled.

I went, You lookin for the whitefish?

He turnt and stared at me like he couldn't tell if I was really there. His mouth was hanging open and you could see his big blobfinger kind of going funny on his lip.

I was still squeezing that rock I had in my hand and I was glad I had it.

After a minute he still didn't say nothing, so I said it again. I went, You lookin for the whitefish?

He just kept staring all googly and dumbfaced and he was moving his blobfinger faster and faster, so I was like, It's *my* fish!

Don't even *think* about stealin it!

But he still didn't say nothing. He just sat in the Red River with the dead water licking his knees. He was like a little kid who falls in a mudpuddle and don't know what to do. Shale Bluehouse used to fall in mudpuddles all the time cause of how his body kind of slumps and don't work right. At the Holy Family Agency I was always pulling him off the floor and helping him out of mudpuddles and stuff.

I was like, You okay, mister?

And in this big dumb voice that sounded like it was coming out of a old rusty lunchbox, he was like, I ain't no mister.

I went, You ain't?

Nuh-uh.

I was like, Then what are you?

And he went, I's Lost.

You a Lost Man?

He looked at me all confused and was like, *Huh?* and he said it like he ain't never heard of no Lost Man in his life, so I was like, You're in the river. The Red River.

I had a red *rib*bon once. Used to carry it in my pocket. Mean Bob taked it. Mean Bob taked it and putted it in the terlet.

River. Red *River.* Not *ribbon.* You're sitting in the *Red River.*

Oh.

What are you doin?

I got losted and I can't find Gil.

Who's Gil?

My bruddah.

Your brother?

Yuh-huh. I got losted when they was putting him in the line.

Puttin him in what line?

The line wif all the udder little kids. I wanted to be in the line, too, but they not taked me cause they said I was too big.

I was like, Lucky you.

And he was like, Huh?

But that would have took too long to explain, so I went, Nothin, and then he started looking at me funny again. His forehead was all twisted up like some kind of big swollen vegetable.

I went, When was the last time you seen him?

Seen who?

Gil.

Gil's my bruddah.

I know that. When was the last time you seen him?

They taked him.

Who?

The mans in the big boots.

The Syndicate?

The *Siddikit.*

It's *Syn*dicate. *Syn*dicate.

The Cindykit.

They took him where?

They taked Gil. They pulled him off the line with their hands. They pulled him the way monsters pull.

I didn't say nothing cause I knowed what that meant. I tried picturing Gil getting dragged away but I couldn't picture his face cause I ain't never seen it before. For some reason I kept seeing *Shale Bluehouse's* face instead.

The giant went, Mean Bob tolted me they was taking him to the Pits but I can't find no Pits.

How old is he?

Mean Bob's like really old. He taked my red ribbon and putted it in the terlet. I think he's firteen or fourteen.

No, Gil. How old is Gil?

Gil's my bruddah and he's eleven in a half.

Then he kind of pointed at my head and went, He's got red hair, too. Then he started crying through his nose again and his crying sounded like a moose blowing in a bottle.

I looked at him sitting there in the water for a minute. His big twisted-up forehead seemed like it was bigger than *three* foreheads.

I was like, How old are you?

And he said, Nineteen.

Nineteen?

Yuh-huh. I be twinny after the Moon comes down.

When's that?

Soon as I build my ellyfant.

Your elephant?

Yuh-huh. His name is *Elton*.

You don't got no elephant.

Yes I do, he said. He's only halfway here, but he's real bright and shiny.

You don't make no sense.

When the Moon comes down and Elton the Ellyfant gets big, I'ma find Gil and the Creature Clouds is gonna stop cryin.

I went, You've been sittin in that water too long. It's makin you stupid.

Then his face kind of went mean and he said, Squash you like a bug on a bubble!

I was like, You couldn't *catch* me.

And he was like, Yuh-huh. My hands is big.

You couldn't catch me if you tried. I hide too good.

Pop you like a bump in a puddle!

I'm hiding right now.

Then he scratched a fishfly off his forehead and wiped the rain out of his eyes and said, You *is*?

I was like, Yep. And you can't even tell.

He started looking at me funny again and went, Gil can hide better than you! He can make his bones smaller! Gil's my bruddah!

You already said that like fifty ga*zill*ion times.

Then he wiped his face again and sneezed and when he sneezed a bunch of fishflies jumped out of the river and the noise of the sneeze and the noise of their wings was so loud it was like it came from the Creature Clouds.

I said, You really got a brother?

Then he went, G-G-G-*Giiiilllll!* and started splashing the water and going ballistic and then, just like that, the giant was crying again and his crying was like the way a moose or a bear would cry if there was still mooses and bears.

I told him to shut up. I was like, *Sh-sh-sh-sh-sh-sh*. Shut up, dummy! You wanna get *clinched*?

He looked at me and scrunched his nose all funny like there was thoughts getting all jammed in his head, and he said, I ain't no *dummy*.

Well, you ain't no brain festival sittin in the water like that.

Then he said, You is mean.

I didn't say nothing after that. I just kind of stood there and watched him scratch the fishflies off of his big forehead and wipe the water out of his eyes.

Then he looked at me with his face all scrunched up, like I was the smallest thing he ever seen, and went, Gil's littler than you.

I was like, So?

And he was like, But he's *faster* and he's got a *dinker*.

I was like, Good for him.

I got a dinker, too.

Big honking wow.

I can pee my name in the dirt if I suck on a pennycopper.

You think that's fancy?

You can't do it.

Wouldn't want to.

You don't got no dinker. You ain't never gonna be no mister.

Don't wanna be no mister!

The last few fishflies made their jumps and sprayed a little water.

I was like, What's your name, dummy?

He was like, I ain't tellin.

Why not?

Cause your eyes is funny.

No they ain't.

Yes they is.

They're pretty. I got Easter egg eyes.

They ain't friendly.

Then I was like, And you're fat as a sow.

No I ain't.

Fat as a sow and slower than a duck with no legs!

Then he started splashing in the water and shouted, You is meaner than Mean Bob and he's the meanest person in the whole white *worlt*!

So I shouted back at him. I went, And you're sitting in the Red River, you big dumb blob festival!

You is mean cause you got fire in your hair!

I ain't mean!

Yes you is!

Then for some reason I was like, Better not touch my whitefish!

He didn't say nothing after I said that. A big gray ghost of fishflies was hovering at the edge of the Bone Trees. You could smell the Red River burning off their wings.

Then, out of nowhere, the giant was like, What's a sow?

For some reason that made me laugh real hard.

He smiled this big lopsided smile and went, When you laugh you sound like Gil.

I do?

Gil's glad and he can roll down a hill and make funfun better than anyone.

Then he stood up and when he reached his full height he was like one of the Bone Trees growing out of the water. He was bigger than any man I ever seen, like at least eight feet.

He stood in the mud and reached into his pocket and pulled out this old dead pennycopper and put it in his mouth and started sucking on it the way you suck on something hard and sour, and then he pushed his pants down, and when he pushed them down he pushed them *all the way down by his ankles* the way a little kid does. Then he flipped at his dinker and started peeing right there in the mud, with the fishflies jumping out of the river and the rain sliding sideways and the Creature Clouds groaning overhead. He looked like a big lost babydoll standing there.

His pee kind of steamed up like a spell rising out of the mud. When he was through there was a little lopsided name on the banks of the Red River. It was all smeared cause of the mud and the rain and all the fishflies that was skittering. It looked about as much like a name as a bunch of smashed crackers in a bowl of chocolate milk.

He was smiling and sucking on his dead pennycopper and looking down at his name with his blobfinger going funny on his lip.

I was like, I can't read that!

He went, It says *Honeycut.*

Honeycut?

He was like, *Yuh-huh-yuh-huh-yuh-huh,* and started walking in these little circles around his name. He didn't even pull his pants up and looked like a big bald confused bear who couldn't find his cave.

I was like, Pull your pants up, Handycoat!

And he was like, It's *Honey*cut! *Honey*cut!

Honeycut!

Then he pulled his pants up and when he pulled them up he still had that big stupid smile on his face. I couldn't help laughing cause of the way he kind of teetered all slow and crooked before he fell backwards in the Red River.

DOOK, DEVIL STICKS,
AND TOO MUCH ALUMINUM

Honeycut took me to his life hole at the edge of the Bone Trees. He said he finded it three halfweeks before, after he lost Gil.

The main room was lit by a few half-dead crooked candles and it was so dark in places you could hardly see the shadows sawing on the walls.

It was cold and clammy and I had to keep my hand over my mouth cause I thought I was going to be sick from the smell. Toward the back it was hot the way a oven gets hot and the smell got even worst. It was like sour milk and old cheese and a thousand gazillion Red River dooks.

All Honeycut had besides the candles and the dooksmells was this old pink blanket that was so ratty-looking it was like some little Undertwelve croaked and then got rolled in the blanket and disappeared. He was still wet so I grabbed the blanket and handed it to him. It looked like a rag or a towel or a little pink newspaper stuck to his shoulder. It had this slippery lining and Honeycut started stroking it all slow and soft.

He kept real close to the edge of the room and started oafing and grunting like there was some kind of cave shark hiding in the shadows.

I was like, You okay, Honeycut?

And he was like, Yuh-huh.

Honeycut just kept reaching for the walls like a big lost bear. For some reason I started thinking of Shale Bluehouse and how he used to keep this little frog in his pocket. We finded the frog in the garden of the Holy Family Agency and it would always pee this green stuff if you pinched its leg. I ain't sure why I thought of that right then, maybe cause of the way Shale would start petting the frog when he was scared.

After I made my way around the room I could finally see what Honeycut was scared about. In the far corner was a big old slop bucket full of dooks. It wasn't no regular slop bucket. When you looked closer you could see that it was one of the Syndicate's *Offertory* buckets. The funny thing was that most of the dooks wasn't even in the bucket. Most of them was on the *floor*. They looked like a bunch of squirrels that got cooked while they was sleeping.

When Honeycut seen me counting the dooks, he got this real lost look on his face, like he got catched stealing candy or something. He wouldn't look at me and kept sucking his blobfinger.

I was like, What's with all that dook, Honeycut?

He wouldn't say nothing. He just stood there. You could see the flames from the candles skittering on his big dumb face. The flameskitters made his face look bigger and dumber than it really was.

You can't live right with all that dook, Honeycut. You could get wormscurvy.

He was like, I ain't got no swervy.

All you gotta do is dump it.

I get skeert . . .

It seemed like he was going to start crying again.

I was like, Scared of what?

The man in terlet.

The man in the *what*?

The *terlet*.

There ain't no man in the toilet.

Yuh-huh. He's real little and he carries a *devil stick*.

A devil stick?

Mean Bob tolted me. Mean Bob said he lives in the terlet and waits for me at night wif his devil stick.

There ain't no man in the toilet, Honeycut. And there ain't no such thing as no devil stick.

Mean Bob said that the man is a ghost and that he floats around in a little ghostboat.

This ain't even no *toilet*! It's a *slop bucket*, you big honking dook festival!

G–G–Gil used to come to the terlet wif me. He would hold my hand so I wouldn't get skeert.

I walked over to the Offertory bucket and grabbed the handle and climbed up through his life hole and dumped it outside. Honeycut followed behind me with his pink blanket hanging off his shoulder. He moved all slow and confused like a big sleepy dog. I let some rain fill the bucket and I sloshed it around and tossed it on the ground.

Honeycut followed me back inside all big and dumb and slow. I put the bucket down and pointed.

There ain't no little man in that bucket, you hear me? Mean Bob's just trying to scare you.

Yuh-huh-yuh-huh-yuh-huh. He'll poke you in the dooker and scream like a *chicken*.

You believe everything people tell you?

Noaf.

Yes you do.

NoIdon'tnoIdon'tnoIdon't.

I reached under Tick Burrowman's garbage bag and pulled my nest out of my pocket. Honeycut stared at it like it was the first time he seen anything like it in his whole life.

He was like, Where'd you find that?

In the Bone Trees. You like it?

Yuh-huh.

Well, if I'm lyin about that man in the slop bucket you can have it.

He looked at me all lost for a second with his blobfinger in his mouth and went, You *promise*?

I promise. Go ahead and look in the bucket.

Then he got this real scared look on his face and kind of leaned over the Offertory bucket.

I was like, Go head.

He had to stoop real low, and he had this face like he was gazing into one of those big magic holes in the *Moon*. He looked at me and then back at the Offertory bucket and then he kind of jabbed his hand inside and pulled it out real quick like there was a snake or some poison in there. Honeycut stood up real tall and kind of smiled real huge and dumb so you could see how he was missing his two bottom teeth in the front.

I was like, *See*?

His smile got bigger and dumber and he stared at me for a long time and it was so long that you could hear the rain on the front of his life hole.

He pointed at my nest and went, Can I *touch* it?

I gave him my nest and he touched it real small and careful and flicked at the twigs. It was so small in his big blobby hand that it looked like something you find in your *shoe*.

After a minute Honeycut gave it back to me and went, What's your name?

I was like, Whensday.

Windy?

Whensday.

He kind of cocked his head funny and said it again. He went, Winsdy?

Whensday Bluehouse.

He said my name over and over to himself real quiet like he

was whispering it to someone else in the room.

Then he went, You gotta bruddah?

I was like, No.

You gotta sissy?

No, I don't got no sister neither.

Then he stuck his blobfinger back on his lip and looked at me real close and went, Windsy?

Whensday.

Winsdy.

I was like, Yeah?

He went, Where do you live?

I don't live nowhere. Not no more.

You wanna live wif Honey?

You ain't clean enough.

Honeycut was like, I be real clean! Real clean, Winsdy! You can be my bruddah.

I ain't no boy!

You can be my sissy!

Ha!

Then, just like that, his hand went up to his face and his lip started quivering and he was crying again.

He was like, Please?

I just watched him like that for a minute. The rain was kind of slooshing on the front of his life hole.

I was like, Don't be a blubber boy, and I tried to say it nice, but that just made it worst.

His crying was real sad and lonesome and that started to make me feel sad and lonesome, too, and I really *didn't* have no place to stay except for maybe in a sodabush or a compost bin and I didn't know how to pick no buckle latch, so I looked him square in the eyes and I told him I'd stay.

I was like, But you can't be makin *dooks* all over the place.

Okayokayokay.

Promise?

I promise.

And we gotta fix this place up and start washin water.

He was wiping his big dumb tears off his face and smearing dirt all over his blobcheeks. He was like, Okayokayo*kay*, again, and just like that, he wasn't crying no more, like someone flipped a switch in his back.

We was quiet for a minute and Honeycut snuffled a few snuffles and smiled this big dumb smile and then he blasted a fart and the sound of his fartblast was like twenty horns being blown by twenty men in a big metal band, and that made both of us laugh and we started kind of honking laughs and going ballistic, and our laugh honks and our ballistickness was bigger than the sound of the rain slooshing on the door and it was bigger than all the fishflies jumping out of the Red River and it was so loud it seemed like it even made all the dooksmells go away for a minute.

After we was quiet again, Honeycut went, Winsdy, can I show you somefin?

I was like, Sure, and then he got all excited and took my hand and when he took it it felt like my hand disappeared into a big warm loaf of bread. He led me to a door at the back of the life hole. Under the door there was this little lightcrack. We was walking all slow and careful the way astronauts walk.

When he opened the door, the lightcrack turnt into a light-*wall* and my eyes got blasted. There was like a gazillion half-dead crooked candles burning and in the middle of the room was this big honking silver blob of something. The light from all the half-dead crooked candles was shining off of it and making it sparkle.

Honeycut walked up to the big silver blob and started smiling and petting it and talking to it real low and tiny.

After a minute I could see that it was supposed to be some kind of *animal*. It had four legs and a back and a head and it was almost as big as Honeycut.

Honeycut kept whispering stuff and petting it all slow and gentle.

I was like, What the heck *is* it?

He went, *Guess*.

It's a bear.

Nuh-uh.

A moose.

What's a moose?

A moose is like a thunderhorse with tennis rackits on its ears.

Noaf!

A hippo.

No.

A ice cream truck.

Winsdy's *mean*!

Well, what *is* it, Dookboy?

It's Elton! Elton the Ellyfant! He's my friend till the end!

Honeycut was so happy his hands was shaking.

I went, Where'd you get him?

I made him. I ain't finished yet. I won't be finished till the Moon comes down.

There was all this aluminum piled in the corners. Some of it was in blobs and some of it was still in the smooth sheets it comes in when it's all rolled in the box. There was like a gazillion blobs of aluminum in that little room.

I was like, Where'd you get all the aluminum, Honeycut?

Honey finded it. Honey finded it when he was looking for Gil.

You finded it where?

Inna wagon. It was real shiny. It was so shiny it was *talkin* to me.

Then I remembered what Mosely Minifield told Tick Burrowman.

I was like, Oh, Honeycut . . .

I still gotta make his ears.

I didn't even want to *think* about what would happen to Honeycut if Astan Loe and the Syndicate finded their aluminum.

Honeycut went, I'ma make his ears so he can hear.

I stared at the half-made elephant for a long time and watched the candleflames dancing silver.

He's gonna help me, Winsdy. He's gonna help me find Gil.

TWO GAZILLION JELLYFISHES

That night Honeycut gave me the pink blanket and he laid next to me on his back. I kept looking over at him cause I ain't never seen such a huge person laying so close. It was like being next to a boat or a big refrigerator.

He smelled like something that gets left in a bucket, but that wasn't *nothing* compared to all the dooks that was in the corner.

I let him hold my nest and he was all smiling and turning it like it was talking to him. Then he reached into his pocket and pulled out these two huge honking teeth. They looked like a pair of *dinosaur* teeth or something.

I was like, What are *them*?

He went, They's Honey's toofs.

Those are *your* teeth?

Yuh-huh-yuh-huh-yuh-huh. Mean Bob hitted Honey in the mouf wif a brick. They felled out but Gil finded em.

He pulled his bottom lip down so I could see these two huge honking gaps where his teeth was supposed to be.

He was like, See? and then he stuffed his two front teeth into the twigs.

I didn't know what to say, so I went, Gee . . . thanks, Honeycut, and patted him on the head. He just smiled this huge toothless smile and oafed a few times.

After he stuffed his teeth in the nest I made sure to take it back cause I was afraid he would smash it. Plus I didn't want him touching it too much cause of my birthpaper. I told him to close his eyes and he did and then I hided it in the corner where there was this little hole in the rock.

Honeycut was like, What's Winsdy doin?

I went, I'm just checkin this candle here . . . to, um, see if there's enough light for the Tooth Fairy.

I knowed about the Tooth Fairy cause of how Shale Bluehouse lost his teeth and how Sister Ricky Toots told him to put them under his pillow and how the next morning there was this little green crayon where the teeth was. Shale Bluehouse got the crayon took away cause he kept trying to eat it, but before they got it I drawed some stuff with it like a bird and this shoe for your toe that I seen in a ballerina book.

Honeycut was completely ballistic about the Tooth Fairy, going, *Ohgoodohgoodohgood*.

It's funny how you could say stuff like that to Honeycut. You could just say it and he'd believe it.

After I hided my nest, we both just laid on our backs and listened to the wind crying. It sounded like a bunch of cats running through the Bone Trees, going *shwhooo-shwhooo-shwhooo*.

Honeycut went, Winsdy?

I was like, Yeah?

He went, You ain't really mean, is you?

Meaner than Mean Bob.

No you ain't.

Meaner than the meanest voodoo fish. Meaner than the meanest mean festival there is.

He was like, *Noyouain'tnoyouain'tnoyouain't!*

After a second I went, No, Honeycut, I ain't really mean.

Then we was quiet for a minute.

He said, Winsdy?

I went, Yeah?

You likes Honey?

I was like, Yeah, Honeycut, I like you. You're okay.

He was like, Honey's okay, and he started smiling again. Honey likes Winsdy, too.

I went, Don't be so *corny*, but I don't think he heard that cause he was too busy smiling and kind of giggling to himself. I thought, What a big honking *boob* festival.

Then Honeycut cleared his throat and said, Once me and Gil putted ketchup on some gum.

I was like, That's gross.

He started laughing real small and quiet. When we ated it looked like blood monsters was killin us.

I didn't say nothing after that and just listened to him oafing his laughs.

After he was through laughing we was quiet for a while. You could still hear the rain on the front of the life hole and the wind bending the tops of the Bone Trees. I was tired and the muscles in my brain felt like they was moving real slow.

Then Honeycut went, Hey, Winsdy, if you want, I could *sing*.

I went, *Sing?*

Yuh-huh.

Sing what?

The Chocolate Funfun Song.

The *who*?

Chocolate Funfun Song. Me and Gil used to sing it all the time.

Okay.

And then he started talking real quick. He went, Chocolate Funfun Song's fun cause you get to run and troublebump and make a *glad* dance.

Well, you don't got to do all that, Honeycut.

Okayokayokay . . .

Then he started singing in this real tiny voice. It was like his song voice was coming out of a little kid who was trapped in his stomach or something.

> *Chocolate funfun, gimme lots of fun*
> *Chocolate funfun, gimme lots of fun*
> *Find a friend on Friday*
> *Find him near the Sun*
> *Eat a box of monkeytoes*

Touch a dragon's tongue
Chocolate funfun, gimme lots of fun
Chocolate funfun, gimme lots of fun
Gil's in the chickenhouse
Honey's on the run
Dooji's by the pickleshack
Elton weighs a ton
Chocolate funfun, gimme lots of fun
Chocolate funfun, gimme lots of fun
River's runnin backwards
Moon just ate the Sun
Biscuits on the table
Apple pie is done

When he finished I clapped and looked over and he was smiling so hard I thought the rest of his teeth was going to pop out. He wanted to sing it again but I told him it was bad luck to sing the same song twice and that it might keep the Tooth Fairy away, even though I ain't sure if that's really true. So we just laid quiet and listened to the rain sliding on the door.

After a while Honeycut's eyes started going all droopy and you could see him fighting sleep.

For some reason I wasn't scared. I thought I would be cause of how I really didn't know Honeycut too good and cause of how it was the first time since Tick Burrowman carried me away in his bodybox that I wasn't going to sleep in his life hole.

And it was the first time I was kind of on my own since the Syndicate clinched me and Shale and all the other kids at the Holy Family Agency. I guess I kept expecting to be scared but it just never came.

Before he fell asleep, Honeycut turnt to me and his eyes got all big and scared-looking. He kind of picked his nose and went, Can I ast you somefin, Winsdy?

I went, Uh-huh.

And he was like, How old is you?

I just looked at him and kind of smiled and I said, Thirty-three, Honeycut. I'm thirty-three.

Then I pulled my sleeve up and showed him the number on my arm. He touched it and kind of smiled, and he was like, Firty-*free*! and I was nodding my head all slow and careful cause part of me felt like it was good for him to think that I was all old and growed-up like that. Part of me thought maybe he wouldn't be so scared all the time if he believed I was a adult.

Honeycut's sleeping was like deadness, and the only thing that moved in that deadness was his blobby chest going *umf-umf-umf.* His body was like a big white blobstove and that was good cause after we pinched all the half-dead crooked candles the life hole went kind of cold and clammy.

At first I couldn't sleep too good cause I was so used to hearing the splittingpicks down in the Pits and Tick Burrowman wrestling with his lungpuddles. I was used to my halfbed and the rain running on the door.

In Honeycut's life hole, the rain kind of *walked* on the door and besides the wind you couldn't hear none of them other sounds.

I kept picturing Honeycut trying to build his elephant and I kept picturing how he finded all that aluminum, and in my mind I kept hearing the collection wagon creaking and it got so loud that it was like that collection wagon was right outside. And Astan Loe was right there with it, sitting on his big thunderhorse, and that thunderhorse's eyes was all black and spooky and Astan Loe had this big electricity stick that he was going to use on Honeycut, and he was holding it so hard that the veins in his hands was popping out like little blue skinsnakes.

And then, for some reason, I started seeing *Tick Burrowman* sitting on that thunderhorse, too. He was sitting right on the back of the saddle and he had his arms around Astan Loe's waist so he wouldn't fall off and he kind of fit up on the thunderhorse real nice cause of how he's all bowlegged and stuff. Him and Astan Loe was kind of smiling and cracking jokes.

All those thoughts made my heart feel small and hard.

And I ain't sure if those hard small feelings had anything to do with it—I couldn't be sure about none of that—but that's when the blood came.

It felt like something was getting torn open inside me and all the muscles in my guts and the muscles underneath my guts and the muscles under*neath* the muscles underneath my guts started pulling tight. It felt like my whole *body* was going ballistic and the buds in my chest was hurting real bad like there was some stones in my boobies. It was like forks and knives and spoons was spinning all around inside me. Like they was spinning faster and faster and their spinning was making everything pull harder and tighter. And the pulling kept getting longer and longer and it was making me feel like I had to curl up into a little knot so that pulling would stop, but it didn't. It didn't stop no matter how hard I curled or knotted and those stones in my boobies was feeling like they was about to *pop right out* and roll away on the floor.

Honeycut just kept sleeping and breathing his blobby breath and I tried to stay as quiet as I could cause I didn't want him to wake up and get all scared and start going ballistic.

Then everything in my pants went kind of warm and wet and I put my hand down there and when I pulled it back up there was all this *blood* on my fingers. You couldn't see it too good cause it was so dark, but you knowed it was blood cause it was kind of sticky and slippery and you could smell the metal in it.

At first I was all shaking and scared cause you can't just have *blood* bleeding out of you like that unless you been bit by a *ditch dog* or stabbed with a *knife*. And you can't have no blood bleeding out of your privacy and expect to feel okay no matter *what* happens.

But then I remembered how this one Bluehouse nun at the Holy Family Agency left the bathroom one day and how I finded this big white thing that was shaped like a blackboard eraser. It was stuck to the top of the toilet seat and I remember how it had this big blood smear in the middle of it and how I took it and showed it to Shale Bluehouse and how we was going to try and trade it to this little kid called Skreety for this rubber chickenhead he finded in one of the garbage cans.

We didn't get far with that bloody white eraser thing cause one of the other Bluehouse Sisters catched us when I stuck it to the top of Shale's head and the Bluehouse Sister took it away and when she took it away Shale Bluehouse asked her what it was and she said that it was a bandage for women cause they make blood every month so their bodies can get ready for making babies.

I didn't understand that cause nuns ain't supposed to make no babies cause of how they got this special love festival with *God* and stuff, and Shale even said that to that Bluehouse Sister, but she just laughed at him and took the white thing away and when she took it away she took it away like we wasn't never going to see nothing like that for the rest of our lives. It was like she was taking it to the *Moon* or something.

So after I smelled that blood on my fingers I got up and pulled on the garbage bag. I felt like I had to walk. I thought walking would take that pulling feeling away. I thought maybe walking would make the blood stop.

Honeycut was fast asleep and dreaming some dream that was making his face look dead.

I walked out into the rain and just stared up through the tops of the Bone Trees.

The Red River was quiet. There wasn't no fishflies jumping and there wasn't no voodoo fishes voodooing and I couldn't see my whitefish whitefishing nowhere.

The rain stopped going sideways, which meant you could see a lot more stuff, like how the tops of the Bone Trees looked like old skeleton hands twisting toward the sky and how the Creature Clouds was all swollen and dark and blacksmeared.

I pulled up the bottom of Tick Burrowman's garbage bag and I took my pants down and all these bloody jellyfishes started swimming out of me. They was red and gloopy and they kind of just blobbed down all soft and quiet. It was like my body was a big long river and the jellyfishes swimmed the whole length of it and now they was tired and all they wanted to do was blob down out of me so they could sleep.

I stood there and watched them swim down for a few minutes. I tried to count them cause I thought using numbers would make it less scary but there was like two ga*zillion* of those jellyfishes swimming out of me. They got all trapped in my legs and glooped on my shoes and the rain started mixing with them so it looked like they was trying to swim away on the ground.

I heard someone coming through the Bone Trees so I pulled my pants up and pushed Tick Burrowman's garbage bag down and ducked into this little sodabush.

Through the branches I could see three Syndicate soldiers running with torches and the torches looked like giant fireflies doing somersaults in the air. You could see that they was carrying electricity sticks too, cause they was kind of throbbing blue. Then there was these three ditch dogs pulling three *more* Syndicate soldiers and you could hear them breathing all hot and nasty underneath their muzzlestraps. It sounded the way fire sounds if you get too close to it.

You could hear one of the Syndicate soldiers going, *Where'd that little bastard go?* and another one was like, *This way!* and the third Syndicate soldier went, *Up through the Bone Trees! Up through the Bone Trees! Get that little bastidge!* and then they disappeared and you could see their torches bobbing and somersaulting into the blackness.

I still had my fist pressed into my privacy and I was about to make a run for Honeycut's life hole when I heard someone else coming. This time there wasn't no torches and there wasn't no electricity sticks. All I could make out was that it was a man and he was walking real slow and he was carrying something and his carrying was kind of lopsided and crooked.

You could hear his shoes sliding over the ground, going *shloo-shloo-shloo*, and you could hear him breathing hard and he was getting so close that you could *smell* him. You could smell him the way you can smell a thunderhorse before you see it.

The blood was still coming and those jellyfishes was still

swimming down. Everything was all gloopy and ballistic but I didn't really care cause I was too scared of getting clinched.

I thought maybe it was another Syndicate soldier carrying a big Offertory bucket or something, like maybe he was trying to find that lost aluminum, but when I looked I couldn't see no black boots and I couldn't see no tail of no greatcoat swooshing.

And then when I looked closer, I could see that the man was carrying a *bodybox*. He had the lid open and he was walking kind of half-folded and bowlegged and he was even singing this little song through his nose. I couldn't tell what the song was at first but it sounded real familiar and then I could feel that song kind of living inside me and that's when I knowed who it was. I could see him real clear now and he was kind of hobbling along the banks of the Red River with his bodybox.

He looked real old right then. He looked a lot older than he ever did in his life hole. That song he was singing through his nose was the same song he sang when he carried me up and away from the Numbering Line. His face looked real tired and sad and I could tell that he was crying.

Tick Burrowman was hobbling along, going *Thirty-three! Thirty-three, where are you, little girl?*

He wasn't wearing no garbage bag and his arms and face was all sticky from the safe jam, and his voice sounded like it was full of tears and those voicetears almost made me want to come out from the sodabush, but something kept telling me to stay. Something inside me knowed that he was just going to make me get into the bodybox so he could take me back to his life hole. And even though that didn't seem like such a horrible thing, something in the small parts of my bones knowed that that woman with the clown makeup was waiting for me in her big black car. I could just see her in the back seat of her car and she was putting more of that white makeup on her face and smoking one of those fancy cigarettes and listening to the kind of music that people with big shiny cars listen to.

And when I thought of that woman taking me away in that big black car, I didn't picture her taking me to a place where I could *live*. I kept imagining her taking me to a *stable* or a *chickenhouse* or some kind of lost *pit* for a Digit Kid.

I kept thinking how she would just keep me locked up in some little metal room for a while, and then when she was ready, she would come and get me and put me on this big honking hospital table and then some doctor would come into the room and steal all of my babymaking parts.

Tick Burrowman was bending real low with the bodybox and his arms was shaking and he was singing that song through his nose and swallowing those tears in his throat, going *Thirty-three, oh, Thirty-three*, over and over and over again.

I watched him for a long time. I watched his little white arms and I watched his crooked old goat legs and I watched how he was trying to keep the rain out of the bodybox, and all of that kind of made me sad. It made me sad cause it was like there wasn't nothing no one could do for Tick Burrowman. It was like God *made* him that way.

Eventually his little lopsided body disappeared along the banks and his disappearing was like something in the sky that gets swallowed by the Creature Clouds.

That's when the rain started going sideways again. And the mist off of the Red River kind of boiled up and you could smell the voodoo fishes.

I fell asleep right there in the sodabush. I fell asleep hard and I fell asleep with my fist pushed into my privacy. That pulling feeling started going numb inside me. Numb like something real big and cold. I felt like I was turning into a snowman. Before I finally fell asleep that's how I seen myself—all white and round and cold, with some black stones for eyes and a carrot for a nose and this big nasty blood stain at my privacy.

Like a big dumb bloody snowman.

It's hard to tell when something's inside you. It's hard to tell cause when you wake up and it's there you don't know what it was like when it wasn't there. You wake up and there's mansmells and oaf-oaf-oafing and moving and the moving is like waves breaking over you and the thing inside you is hard and it hurts and it's like something with a motor pushing through you and the only thing you can think of is how that pushing is like the thunder moving through the Creature Clouds and the rain moving through the Bone Trees and the fishflies moving through the Pits, and you can't tell what it is cause you wasn't awake when it went in when it went in when it went inside you all hard and tight and bloody. You wasn't awake and everything's still numb cause of the pulling and the blood and the jellyfishes swimming and the knots you was trying to make with your body and the knots and the knots and the knots you was trying to make with your body. But then you do wake up, you do wake up, you wake up and there's a man attached to that thing inside you and the man's got mansmells and his mansmells is hot and thick and he's oaf-oaf-oafing and push-push-pushing and breaking those waves and it's like buildings is falling and the Creature Clouds is laughing at you and the night is running in you all dark and hard and numb and there's so much blood it's like everything's turnt into the Red River and all those jellyfishes is swimming down and all the blood in my body is the water and I'm just a little boat floating, I'm just a little boat floating, I'm just a little boat, and now it's like I'm a little bodybox full of blood and those waves keep breaking over me and those mansmells keep coming and the man attached to that thing inside me is big and strong the way a thunderhorse is strong and he's oaf-oaf-oafing and push-push-pushing and he's wearing a greatcoat and I can see the falcon tail of his greatcoat swooshing and now I can see his big black boots, his big black boots, his big black boots, and now it's like I ain't even there no more, like I ain't even there no more, like I ain't even there. It's like I've turnt into a little white snowbird and I'm kind of floating over that sodabush and I can see my face before I became a snowbird and I can see my little bloody legs before I became a snowbird and I can see all those jellyfishes swimming out of me and I can see how curly and red my hair is, how curly and red my hair is, how curly and red I am. And I can see that man push-push-pushing, push-push-pushing, push-push-pushing his mansmells inside of me. But I can't feel nothing no more cause of how I'm floating above it all, how I'm floating above it all, how I'm floating above, how I'm floating. And my heart is like a stone in my chest and it's like I got three stones in my chest, and everything's numb and I feel like I'm fading, I feel like I'm fading, like I'm fading, I'm fading . . .

DEAD MAN

When I waked up, Honeycut was kneeling beside me and he was petting my hair and there was all these half-dead crooked candles burning small and clean and their candle-flames was sawing and bending and flickering like little stars trying to talk.

Honeycut was all sad and lonesome-looking and after he stopped petting my hair he started rocking back and forth and rubbing his arms like he was cold. His face was kind of dead and spooky and every time he turnt to me he would start to open his mouth but he couldn't say nothing. He would open it so hard you could *hear* how the words was all trapped in his throat.

It felt like all my blood was missing, like it bleeded out of me the way air leaks out of a balloon. That's what I felt like—a little dead balloon. I was shaking and I had both fists pressed into my privacy and I was more thirsty than I ever been in my life.

I seen the bucket in the corner and there was some water in it that looked all dark and black and smooth like silk. There was a bunch of lit candles around it, and you could see candle-flames dancing on the skin of the water.

Honeycut walked over to the bucket and cupped some half-washed water in his hands and poured it into my mouth. The water was hot and smelled funny, but it was good to drink cause of how thirsty I was. I was so thirsty I could have drinked straight out of the Red River.

I knowed it wasn't no dream no more when I seen the man. He was laying in the corner and he looked like a man who had walked a gazillion miles and then got tired and just laid down and fell asleep. He was wearing a greatcoat and big black Syndicate boots and the buttons in his pants was so shiny you could see the candleflames dancing in them. But he wasn't moving none. He was laying on his back but when you looked at his head all you could see was the *back of his hair* and the *back of his neck*. Everything started going all tight and hard and I could feel a hurt in me like a piece of metal. And that metal was turning in my guts and it was turning under my guts and it was turning under the guts under my guts and it was kind of turning in my privacy, too.

When I was finished drinking out of Honeycut's hand I was like, Who's that, Honeycut?

He was tryin to hurt. He was tryin to make a hole in Winsdy. He was tryin to make Winsdy disappear.

I looked over at the man and then I felt my fists and how they was pressed into my privacy real tight and I knowed what happened.

He was tryin to make a *hole* in Winsdy so Honeycut maked

him *stop*. Honeycut maked him stop real *good* . . .

I was hot and sweaty and all the blood in my fists was making my fingers sticky and you could smell it and that man in the corner could smell it too and he came to the sodabush while I was sleeping and put it inside me cause it's the metal in your blood that makes that happen.

There was a small trunk turnt on its side. At first I thought it was another man laying there.

Honeycut walked over to it and lifted the lid and inside the trunk was all these cans of food. He grabbed a can and when he grabbed it the can kind of disappeared into his hand.

Where'd you get that?

Honeycut finded it when he stop the *man*. He give it to us. He said we could *have* it.

That's when Honeycut started crying. His crying was like twenty men crying and it was so loud it shaked the walls in the life hole. Even though the walls was rocks and they probably ain't been shaked in like a gazillion years, they started vibrating like crazy.

I rolled out of the pink blanket and runned over to the man and started kicking him. I kicked him in the ribs and I kicked him in the arms and I kicked him in the head and I kicked him in his privacy and my kicking was like twenty legs kicking and I didn't care that there was still jellyfishes swimming out of me and I didn't care that everything was kind of numb and lost-feeling and I didn't care that my arms and legs was shaking like there was a bunch of electricity wires going ballistic in my bones. It felt like the more I kicked the more that hole he made in my privacy would turn into a non-hole.

After a while I stopped kicking cause Honeycut went all quiet and just sat down in the middle of the life hole like a big lost bear. I sat down too—right there next to the dead man. I just sat cause it felt like the world would stop. I could smell his mansmells and I could see the hair on his arms but I couldn't see his mouth or his nose or his eyes cause of how his head was facing the floor. So I reached over and turnt his head around. I turnt his head around cause I wanted to see. I wanted to see all those faceparts and I wanted them to burn in my brain so I would always remember. I wanted them to burn the way matches burn. But when I turnt his head I knowed I wouldn't have to cause I already knowed them. I already knowed them the same way you know about the poison in the rain before it burns you.

It was Second Staff Brown and his mouth was open and his eyes was as wide as eggs and he had this look on his face like he just seen something amazing. Like he seen a slit of silver in the Creature Clouds. Like he seen God doing something in a tree.

I reached into my pants and grabbed the rest of that cheese that I still had from Tick Burrowman's cupboard. For some reason I stuffed the cheese right into his mouth. I stuffed it hard and I stuffed it till I couldn't stuff it no more. Then I took the stubs of two candles and I placed them over his eyes.

After that I looked over at Honeycut.

I was like, At least we got food.

Yuh-huh.

We got plenty of food . . . And Elton.

Elton the Ellyfant. He's my *friend*.

But we don't got no safe jam. And we gotta get you a garbage bag.

I knowed there was lots of stuff we needed. Like we needed to get rid of the body and we needed more candles and we needed to find some way to open those cans of food. And I needed to find a way to stop those jellyfishes from jellyfishing out of me.

Honeycut stood up real tall and kind of pushed away from the wall.

I'ma go talk to Elton.

I was like, Okay, even though I really didn't want him going nowhere.

Honeycut walked to the back and disappeared into that room with all the aluminum foil. I just laid there and listened to the rain. I couldn't sleep. It felt like I wouldn't be able to sleep for a long time. It felt like my eyes was made of metal and that they wouldn't never close right again.

FOUR HUNDRED AND THIRTY-SEVEN VOLTS OF JUNGLE LOVE

We kept his pants and his boots. We kept his shirt and his socks. We kept his belt and his comb and his little tin of safe jam.

We kept his greatcoat.

After we folded everything and stacked it in a neat pile, me and Honeycut rolled Second Staff Brown in the pink blanket and Honeycut lifted him over his shoulder and carried him out into the rain.

I thought about all those times Second Staff Brown came to Tick Burrowman's life hole to check on the bodyboxes and how he always looked clean and strong, and I thought about how he talked about the sliding rain and how he always tried to not-talk about what was going on down in the Pits. But then I started remembering what he was doing to me in the sodabush and I couldn't feel nothing but deadness.

Deadness and numbness and that snowman cold.

I lit the rest of the candles cause I thought lighting them would take that snowman feeling away. Most of them was getting pretty small cause of all the water we was washing and their smallness made the shadows climb lower and wider on the walls. It looked like big long spooky cats was crawling everywhere.

I kept thinking about Honeycut down by the Red River. I was hoping that he would walk into the water and just drop Second Staff Brown right in the middle all ploppy and croaked. In my mind I could see the body sinking down through the water like a big old carpart, and then I could see it glunking at the bottom all slow and swollen.

I took one of the candles and dripped a waxblob and scratched a Ninety-three in the middle.

It was the ninety-third doubleday of rain and everything had changed. It's funny how two days can make everything go all crazy. And it's even funnier how *people* can change in those two days. It's like ditch dogs turning into werewolves and snakes into birds. That stuff don't happen too often, but when it does you better be ready cause a bird can't change back to no snake once it's got wings and some feathers. I guess Nature can just go all crazy and ballistic on you when you ain't looking. That's the way God makes it and you don't got no choice but to just sit on the floor and wait for something else to happen.

That's what I was thinking about when I heard the knock on the front of Honeycut's life hole. At first it was just one knock. It sounded all croaked and tiny like someone throwed a dead pennycopper up against the door. After the knock you could hear the wind whistling and the trees bending and the groans groaning in the Creature Clouds.

And then there was two knocks and they sounded a little bigger like maybe they was some quartersilvers instead of a pennycopper.

Then there was three and four and five quartersilver knocks with nothing in between them.

I got off the floor and made my way to the front of the life hole. It was like I was in a dream and something was pulling me to the front of the life hole—something like a big invisible hand. There was more knocking and then I heard this little kid's voice going, *Open the door, lemme in! Lemme in, galldangitall!*

You never know who's on the other side of a life hole. It could be a Syndicate soldier holding a electricity stick next to some kid who got clinched. Sometimes they do that to lure out the unclinched Undertwelves.

I was like, Let *who* in?

And the voice was like, *Me*, G!

Who's *Me*?

Me's *me*!

You gotta name?

Course I gotta name, but I ain't gonna tellya!

Then you can stay out there all *double*day for all I care.

Lemme in, galldangitall! The Blobfish is comin!

The what?

The *Blob*fish! He's like twelve feet tall. He's comin to eat me! He was in the river and he's comin thisaway!

I was like, There ain't no Blobfish in the river!

Yes there *is*, G!

G?

He had a man. Man was naked as a stick. Blobfish was warshin him right in the Red River. He was warshin him so he could *eat* him!

I went, How old are you? You a Undertwelve?

Whaddaya think? Open the door, G. Hurry up!

I was like, You was down in the Pits?

Yeah.

You got a digit to prove it?

Course I got a digit.

What number they give you?

Four thirty-seven.

Four hundred and thirty-seven?

Yeah, G. *Four thirty-seven.* You got a problem with that?

You musta went down late.

Late, *nothin*. They're in the seven hunnerts now.

I didn't say nothing for a minute. I tried picturing all those kids down there but it made me sleepy so I stopped.

I went, You sick?

I ain't sick.

You sure?

Yeah, G. I'm sure.

You don't got no hotspots?

I don't got *nothin*, G.

You could hear the wind and you could hear the rain and you could hear the Bone Trees creaking like a big lost pirate ship.

I kind of got all sad cause I kept seeing Shale Bluehouse and how his face was in the Numbering Line, how it looked all old and spooky and how that didn't make no sense cause of how he's still a little kid and all . . .

You gonna open the door? I said I ain't sick!

He started knocking and kicking and going ballistic and I think I even heard him start to cry.

I don't know why I asked this but I did. I was like, Still rainin out there?

Course it's still rainin, G! Stuff burns, too.

I went, You alone?

Course I'm alone, galldangitall! Can't get nowhere unless you's alone! Shit!

Stop swearin!

Shooo!

You swear again and I ain't opening this door, you hear me?

He was like, Okay, cool! It's cool, G!

When I opened the door the rain was sideways. The tops of the Bone Trees looked like a bunch of black snakes hissing toward the sky and the Creature Clouds had doubled their bellies and this little kid was standing in the entrance. He was wet as a fish and shivering and his teeth was chattering like there was some electricity running in his bones. He had this crazy dark hair that looked like a smashed blackbird on his head. He just stood there wiping the rain out of his eyes and looking over his shoulder all nervous and skittery. He was so pale it was like he got imagined by the Moon. He wasn't wearing no plastic and he didn't have no safe jam slimed on his skin and his T-shirt was brown with mud and slops and other stuff that I couldn't even name and there was all these white quickdust smears on his mismatched shoes. One shoe was kind of brown and small and the other shoe was blue and chubby and looked like it belonged to his older brother. There was quickdust smears on his pantlegs, too.

I was like, Well, if you're comin in, come in, and then he kind of *runned* into Honeycut's life hole like he was getting chased by a tor*n*ado or something.

I closed the door behind him and he runned to the middle of the life hole and kneeled down in front of a bunch of candles and pulled his shirt off. There was little welts all over his body and a bunch of scratches on his chest and hands. I couldn't tell if the welts was from the rain or if they was hotspots.

He waved the heat toward his chest all frantic and crazy. You could see his ribs and the little muscles muscling in his back and you could see the three digits on his left shoulder. 437. They was all scabby and gross and you could tell he'd been picking at them cause of all the pus.

After a minute he stopped waving the heat toward him and he just kneeled real still with his hands over the candleflames.

His fingers was spread all careful like he was praying through his palms.

I grabbed the Offertory bucket and walked over to where he was kneeling and offered him some washed water and he took the bucket in his hands and started drinking the way a dog drinks from a mudpuddle if it ain't drinked all doubleday. His throat jumped and jiggled and glurped, he drinked so much.

I was like, Not so *much*, kid!

I had to snatch the bucket away from him so me and Honeycut would have some water for later. He fought for it, too, but then he let go when he seen that even though I'm a girl I was stronger than his skinnyfaced butt. His little bony chest was leaping and his eyes looked like they was going to pop to blackness right in his head.

I went, Last night down by the river I seen some Syndicate soldiers goin for a clinch. You're the one they was chasin, ain't you?

He went, Galldangin *ditch dogs*. I'm sick of them fiendin-ass gutter mutts. Then he took a big glurp of air and went, *There's a blobfishintheriver . . . ablobfishIswear . . .* , and then he couldn't catch his breath. I thought he was going to explode right there in the middle of Honeycut's life hole.

That's when I took him by the shoulders and shaked him real hard. I think I shaked him so hard the air flew right out of his lungbags cause he stopped talking and just stared at me with his mouth open.

I was like, Calm *down*, Hyperboy!

He kept snuffling and taking big gulps of air and in between two gulps he went, That *ain't* . . . my *name*.

And I was like, Well, what is it, then?

Oakley.

Oakley?

That's right. Oakley *Brown*house.

You was at the Holy Family Agency?

He nodded and kept glurping air.

I was like, I was there, too! I'm a Bluehouse! Then, for some reason I was like, What kinda name is Oakley?

That's a galldangin *good* name is what that is!

Sounds like a furniture store.

He went, What's *your* name—Judy Cruisecontrol or somethin?

Ha!

Bet it ain't as dope as mine.

I was like, Whensday.

He looked at me funny and went, *Whens*day?

I nodded and went, Whensday Bluehouse.

That ain't no name.

More of a name than yours.

That's like one of those old days of the week, G.

Stop calling me G.

Down in the Pits they don't even *use* the days of the

week no more.

What do they use?

Oneday, Twoday, Threeday. That's a halfweek. Fourday, Fiveday, Sixday. That's one, too. You should change your name to Threeday.

I should squeeze your arm till your hand pops off, too.

I'm just sayin.

Then for some reason I was like, Lots of kids down in the Pits, huh?

Hells yeah. Can't even count em no more.

I tried to not-picture the kids but I kept seeing all those digits. I pointed at his arm and went, You like your number?

He kind of raised his elbow so he could see his shoulder and went, Four hunnert thirty-seven volts of jungle *love*, G.

I was like, *Volts*! I got more volts in my *shoe*laces!

Any time you're ready for Oakley Brownhouse's four hunnert thirty-seven volts of jungle *love* you just let him know.

The closest thing you ever been to a jungle is the *Bone* Trees!

Shooo. Come a little closer and I'll show you somethin.

I was like, You prolly ain't even *ten*.

And he was like, Yes I is.

No you ain't, little Oakley Brownmouse.

I knowed that would get him going, and it did. He went, It's *house*, G! Brown*house*!

Ain't ten, ain't ten, ain't ten, I said.

Am too am too am too!

Liars don't get to stay here!

That shut him up. His mouth turnt into this little dumb hole again. After he was quiet for a second, he swallowed some air and went, Nine in a half. Ten. Same differnts.

You're just a kid.

Kid *this*, he said, and grabbed his crotch like he really had something down there.

I was like, You're crazy.

Crazy's better than dead, G.

He tried to drink from the bucket again but I snatched it away and put it the corner. When I turnt around Oakley Brownhouse was staring at me all ugly and scrunchnosed.

What's with your cooterfish?

I said, My *what*?

You're bleedin like a stuck chicken.

I put my fist in front of my privacy and kind of sat down.

He was like, Do it hurt?

It's just kind of numb is all.

Damn, G.

Whensday. My name is *Whensday*. Not G!

Damn, Wesley . . .

We didn't say nothing for a minute. His hands was spread over the candleflames and you could see these little blue veins snaking in the tops of his fingers. I think they was the smallest veins I ever seen.

You could still hear the rain on the front of the life hole. I was starting to really worry about Honeycut.

I looked at Oakley Brownhouse for a minute and went, Hey, Oakley Brownhouse.

Hey what?

Down in the Pits . . .

. . . Yeah?

You didn't know no little kid called Shale, did you?

. . . Nope.

Bluehouse kid. Left leg don't work right. Falls down a lot.

Didn't know no one like that. Wasn't hardly no Bluehouse kids *down* there.

Big bushy hair. Keeps a frog in his pocket.

Didn't see no frogs in nobody's pocket.

Big bushy *ballistic* hair. Biggest honking hair you'll ever see.

Didn't see nothin like that, G. Big hair don't mean nothin no more noway.

How come?

Cause they started shavin heads.

They shave your head?

Them Syndicate suckers was shavin everyone. They think the Buckfrost bugs sleep in your hair.

Girls, too?

Girls is part of everyone, ain't they? Shoo, that's how come I skated.

I was like, You runned away cause they was gonna

shave your *head*?

First they take your hair and then it's everything else. He hit himself in the chest a few times and went, Oakley Brownhouse ain't no *sucker*.

Then there was all these new sounds from the wind, like a bunch of monsters screaming. And after the screaming you could hear this kind of spooky gurgling in the Creature Clouds.

After a minute I was like, How'd you get away?

He was like, How you *think*? I hided in one of them body-boxes.

For some reason I was like, Cool.

Cool nothin. Had to hide in that thing for damn near two *hours*. When they wasn't lookin I skated, G. Climbed right up the rock ladder. That's how I got all these scratches on my chest. Got my ass bit up by one of them ditch dogs, too, see?

Oakley Brownhouse took his pants down and showed me his one little butt cheek that had this big red bite mark on it. He pulled his pants up real fast and kind of kneeled back down and went, But I kicked his nuts in.

I went, Does it hurt?

Everything hurts a little, G. Shoulda heard that ditch dog yelp when I blasted him, though. Bet his nuts is *still* rollin around.

We didn't say nothing for a minute and then I went, Was it empty?

Was what empty?

That bodybox.

Hells no.

There was someone in it?

Course there was. That's what them things is down there for, G.

Who was it?

Some little baldy. Think it was a hooker cause her titties was kind of stickin out. But you can't even tell between dudes and hookers now cause of everyone bein bald.

Dudes and *hookers*?

Dudes and hookers. Boys and girls, G. B's and G's. You know what I'm sayin.

What was it like hidin in that box?

Stunk all to hell. Smelled like chicken guts.

I thought about that little girl and how she didn't have no hair. I thought of that and it made me feel hot and small.

I went, You're the first one I seen.

First one you seen *what*?

Get away.

You mean you didn't get away?

I never went down.

You didn't?

I shaked my head.

He went, You oldern twelve?

I'm eleven.

They didn't put no number on you?

I rolled my sleeve up and showed him my Thirty-three. He touched it and was like, Damn, G. You went down *early*.

I covered my Thirty-three and went, This man came and pulled me off the line.

You a *Futurist*?

No. They hired him to make the bodyboxes. He pulled me off the line cause he needed to show them how a Digit Kid could fit inside.

How come he chose you?

I don't know. Never asked him.

He went, You lucky.

I didn't say nothing.

Lucky as a *wishbone*. I should call you Lucky G.

Then, for some reason, I was like, You don't got no friends, do you?

And he was like, I don't got no *friends*?

You was prolly all lonely down in the Pits.

You don't know.

Cursin like that. Big honkin chip on your shoulder.

I got friends!

Ha!

I do!

Who?

. . . This one kid.

What kid.

I ain't tellin.

Cause he ain't real.

Realer than *you*, you red-headed hooker!

Yeah, sure. Just like that Blobfish in the river.

He was like, There *is* a Blobfish, okay!?

I kind of smiled and went, Uh-huh.

There *is* a blobfish and I *did* have a friend in the Pits. And I ain't no sucker.

I was like, Imaginary friends ain't never really there, Oakley Brunsonhouse!

He went, *Brown*house!

I was like, It's cool, G, just to see what he would do, but all he did was look at me with his face twisted up like his toilet muscles was going squishy.

Then he started picking at his shoulder and just when I thought we was going to be quiet for a minute he went, His name was *Gil*, okay! and he started crying and his crying was all silent and his face was all scrunched into itself like it got stuck that way. He cried like it was the first time he ever cried over anything in his little lost life.

I almost walked over and touched Oakley Brownhouse's face just to make it start moving regular again, but I didn't. Instead, for some reason, right when I started reaching my hand out, I kind of *hit* him. I don't know why I did that. It was all crazy and ballistic-feeling, and I didn't even hit him that *hard*, but I hit him with my fist and when I looked at my fist after I hit him it was all red from how hard I was squeezing my fingers together.

I ain't never really hit no little kid before. Somehow it kind of felt like I hit *myself*, though, and that's like one of the spookiest, most ballistic feelings you'll ever have.

After that, Oakley Brownhouse stopped crying and sort of started touching his face all small and careful. He looked real lost and sad.

I couldn't hear nothing cause it was like I had all this noise in my head. There wasn't no wind and there wasn't no rain and there wasn't no trees bending. It was like the noise was so loud that it killed all the other sounds.

It was like everything that happened had froze me. I just stood there with my fist pressed against my privacy. I almost forgot about the jellyfishes.

When he started to talk you could hear how tears was trapped in his throat. I felt like I wanted to touch him, but I couldn't. I couldn't cause I was afraid I would hit him again.

Oakley Brownhouse swallowed his tears and went, His name was Gil and he's dead, okay? He's dead.

ENTER THE BLOBFISH

*un, G! Run!*

I waked up to Oakley Brownhouse's little voice screaming. My face was itchy from sleeping on the greatcoat and my shoulders was all cramped and tired from pressing my fists into my privacy.

It's the Blobfish, G! It's the Blobfish!

His voice was like some glass breaking. When I looked up, Honeycut was standing over me, his face all big and soft and his eyes shiny with tears. He was holding my whitefish. It looked like a little rubber toy in his hand.

He was talkin to me, Winsdy. He tolted Honey he wanted to go *home* wif him. He said he wanted to see *Winsdy.*

Run for your life, G! Run for your life!

I touched the fish. It was cold and wet and slippery and its eye looked like a doll's eye.

Honeycut was like, Can we *keep* it?

I nodded and went, We can keep it. We'll keep it for good luck.

Winsdy ain't mad at Honey, is she?

No, Honeycut. I ain't mad at you.

After he put my whitefish down, he touched my hair. It felt

nice. Even though his hand smelled all gross and boogery from the Red River it still felt nice.

I went, Anyone see you?

Nuh-uh.

You sure?

Yuh-huh. Honey's sure. He don't see *nobody*.

Then he got up and oafed to the back of the life hole with the whitefish.

I was like, Where you goin, Honeycut?

I'ma talk to *Elton*.

I got up and followed cause I knowed Oakley Brownhouse would go completely ballistic when he seen Honeycut. I had to move real slow cause of all the pulling and knotting and the jellyfishes jellyfishing. Those snowman feelings was still going numb inside.

When we opened the door to the back room, half the crooked candles was pinched and Oakley Brownhouse was hiding under Honeycut's elephant and he was shaking and whimpering like a little lost dog. You could hear his teeth chattering like he ate a bunch of *icicles* or something.

When he seen Honeycut he went, *Aaaaaaaaahhhhhhhhh!*

And when Honeycut seen Oakley Brownhouse he was like, *Aaaaaaaaahhhhhhhh!*

Then they both screamed at the same time and their screaming was so loud it was like ten men and ten little Undertwelve *super*screams.

I clapped my hands together a bunch of times and went, Shut up, you big boob festivals!

They both stared at me all open-mouthed and spookfaced like *I* was the crazy one.

Oakley Brownhouse went, *Blobfish alert! Blobfish alert! Blobfish's gonna attack me with that fish!*

I was like, No he ain't.

And Honeycut went, No I ain't.

To Oakley Brownhouse I went, He ain't no Blobfish! Stop bein such a *sissychicken*, but he just stayed under the half-made elephant like he was afraid he would get struck by lightning or swallowed by a tornado or something.

Honeycut went, I ain't no bobfish.

I went, See? Blobfishes can't speak. And they're scared of life holes, right, Honeycut?

Honeycut was like, Yuh-huh. Bobfishes can't speak.

To Oakley Brownhouse I went, See? He don't even know what a blobfish *is*.

Then Honeycut scratched his head and went, Who's he, Winsdy?

A little chickenhead lookin for a chickenhouse.

Oakley Brownhouse was like, I ain't no chickenhead!

Just a little lost chickenhead.

I ain't no chickenhead and I ain't lost!

Honeycut was like, I is.

And then I went, Me too, and then we all sort of looked at

each other for a second and I was like, *We're all lost!*

Then Oakley Brownhouse went, You think I'm some kinda sucker? and he said it all mean to me like *I* was the Blobfish.

I went, Yeah, Oakley Brunsonhouse ain't no sucker, you hear? and I made my face all ballistic and crazy and that made Honeycut smile this big oafy smile and then me and Honeycut started laughing and our laughter was like ten men and ten Undertwelve girl laughs, and just when it started to turn into *twenty* men and *twenty* Undertwelve girl laughs, Oakley Brownhouse started *crying*, and his crying was all silent and scrunchfaced and you could see all his teeth which was gross and gloopy with spit and rain and Shelf dirt.

I was like, What's wrong with you, Oakley Brownhouse? but he couldn't answer at first cause of all the gloop in his mouth. Me and Honeycut just kept laughing.

After a minute Oakley Brownhouse was like, I crapped my pants, G! I crapped my galldangin pants!

GIL

I tried rinsing the dooks out of Oakley Brownhouse's pants, but it didn't work so I gave him Second Staff Brown's Syndicate slacks. He cinched the belt real tight so they wouldn't fall down, but they didn't look too bad once the cuffs was folded.

The whitefish was stinking real bad so when Honeycut wasn't looking I took it outside and buried it. What was funny was that he didn't never ask about the whitefish again. Even though he's nineteen, all you got to do with Honeycut is start talking about the Tooth Fairy or Elton the Elephant, and he gets so excited he forgets about stuff.

Back in the life hole I pulled out three cans from the trunk. Honeycut poked holes through the tops with the corner of Second Staff Brown's belt buckle and squeezed the beans and franks through the holes. We ate them cold with our fingers. All you could hear was our hungergrunts and hungergroans. I thought Oakley Brownhouse was going to cut his fingers off trying to fish out the inside of the can.

After Honeycut put his can down, Oakley Brownhouse snatched it and tried to squeeze out the last bits. His eyes was all ballistic and desperate and he looked like a *rat*.

When we was finished I took the cans outside and rinsed them in the rain and brought them back in and stacked them in the corner.

We sat still for a while and listened to the rain walking on the door.

Then Oakley Brownhouse farted real loud and tried to blame it on Honeycut.

I was like, That was *you*, Oakley Brownhouse.

He went, No it *wasn't*, G. *Blobfish* dealt that one.

I just shaked my head and we went quiet again. Honeycut kept wiggling his toes and kind of trying to talk to them like they was his little tiny toefriends or something. He wasn't making no real words but you could hear him trying to be private.

After a while Oakley Brownhouse turnt to Honeycut and went, So what's your name, B?

Honeycut looked at him all lost and confused.

I went, His name is Honeycut.

Honeycut just sat there talking to his toes.

Oakley Brownhouse went, He don't got no last name?

Honeycut looked up and went, I got a last name. Greenhouse.

I was like, Honeycut *Greenhouse*?

Honeycut went, Yuh-huh.

You was at the Holy Family Agency, too?

He nodded and I was like, I'm a *Bluehouse*. Me and Shale!

And Frogface over there's a *Brownhouse*! We're *all* Holy Family!

Nobody said nothing after that. We was *all* farting from the beans, but Oakley Brownhouse was still trying to blame his on me and Honeycut. And what was funny was *his* fartblasts sounded like someone was dragging a big honking *piano* across the floor.

While Honeycut was in the back room, Oakley Brownhouse asked me for another can of beans and franks.

I was like, No way, Spazzboy!

I told him that we only had enough to eat one can each a doubleday. Oakley Brownhouse called me a cheap hooker and said galldangitall and twisted his face all funny and started making this little muscle in his arm like he was trying to scare me or something.

I was like, What's that, a bug bite?

Broke a kid's arm once.

Oh, really?

Wouldn't do what I said, so I snapped it in half.

You couldn't break a *pencil* with those dinky arms of yours!

You're lucky.

I went, Lucky for what?

He went, You're just lucky, okay? and then he released his little musclebump and started touching it like it hurt.

We was quiet and kept trying to not-look at each other. Oakley Brownhouse rubbed his shoulders like they was cold and started rocking back and forth. After a while his rocking got slower and he laid down and fell asleep. He snored for a minute and then he started talking. At first you couldn't understand nothing he was saying, but then his words started coming slower. He was going, *Gil. Hey, B. We gonna do it tonight? We gonna do it, Gil?* Then he was like, *I ain't scared, Gil. I ain't scared . . .*

I tried to slip the pink blanket under his head but it was shaking too much. All of the sudden he sprang to his feet like a bunch of bees bited him in the butt. He cursed all ballistic and crazy and started walking in circles. I didn't say nothing and just watched him walk. He had this look on his face like his toilet muscles was all stopped up. After a while he sat back down.

I went, You was talkin in your sleep.

No I wasn't.

Yes you was.

Only sissies talk in their sleep. I ain't no sissy.

I went, You was talkin to Gil.

He was like, I was? and he had this real scared look on his face.

That's when I told him about how Gil was Honeycut's little brother.

He was like, *Damn.*

I went, I know, Oakley Brownhouse. *Damn.*

Then I scraped wax off the floor and while I did that I told

Oakley Brownhouse how Honeycut was building his elephant cause he thought the elephant would help him find Gil.

Oakley Brownhouse was like, *Seriously?*

Seriously.

He ain't too swift, is he?

I was like, Sometimes it ain't just about bein swift, Boobhead.

Then he told me I was like seven kinds of sensitive and called me G again.

I told Oakley Brownhouse that if Honeycut finded out Gil was dead his heart would break so hard that you could hear it the same way you can hear lightning and thunderclaps. I sat on the greatcoat and pulled my knees into my chest.

Oakley Brownhouse was staring off all blank and flatfaced. I was like, So what happened to Gil, anyways?

All I know is he got sick.

He got Blackfrost?

I don't know about no Buckfrost.

*Black*frost.

Whatever. They say he got sick cause he wouldn't eat.

Why wouldn't he eat?

Cause he thought they was tryin to poison us.

Was they?

I don't know, G. Sometimes my stomach didn't feel too good.

Poison you how?

Gil thought they was puttin glass in our food. Crushin up old lightbulbs and stuff. He mighta been right, too. I waked up with blood in my mouth lotsa times. All warm and thick like wormpiss or somethin.

I pictured Oakley Brownhouse with a bunch of blood bleeding from his mouth. I shouldn't have done that cause then I couldn't look at him without seeing it.

I went, What kind of food was they givin you?

They started us out on this stuff they called cornslop.

Did it taste good?

Taste *good*? That stuff tasted *turble*.

Like a pencil dipped in airplane glue?

You had some?

Around here they call it the mush. Syndicate drops it off every Oldmonday.

Sometimes I thought I'd ruther eat my own hand.

I went, Tastes okay if you melt some cheese in it.

Yeah, well, we didn't have no *cheese*, Cheesy G.

I guess I shouldn't have said that. I guess I wasn't thinking.

Then Oakley Brownhouse scratched at the scab on his shoulder and went, When the cornslop ran out they started feedin us dog food.

Dog food!

Hells yeah. Straight outta the can, G. They didn't even give us no spoons, nuther. Some kids got right down on their hands and knees like they was *chihuahuas* and shit.

You ate it?

Course I ate it. Wasn't nothin else *to* eat.

That's how come you like them beans so much.

Them beans taste like something you eat in a fancy *restaurant* compared to the crap they was forcin down our throats.

No wonder you wanted another can. Poor little starved boy.

I ain't no boy!

Poor little starved Digit Kid. Makin you eat dog food like that.

You eat enough Alpo and that stuff'll make you hungry for *spinnich*, I ain't lyin.

For some reason I was like, You been fartin like a hog, Oakley Brownhouse.

And you ain't, G?

I looked at him for a minute and went, Can't you say my name?

He went, Huh?

My name is Whensday. Can't you say it?

I can say it.

I ain't heard it yet.

Then he said, I can say it, again, but he never said it. Instead, he went, Threeday and shit, under his breath and started picking at his scab again.

Then he lifted his T-shirt and scratched his chest and coughed a little. You could see how his ribs was kind of pressing through his skin.

After he scratched the scab some more, he went, I'm tellin you, G, them Syndicate bastards was always tryin out stuff on us.

Stuff like what?

Once, after we got done pickin this big-ass rock down to nothin they gave us a pogo stick and said whoever could jump the longest would get to go back to Holy Family.

What happened?

About ten of us tried it. I couldn't get past thirty jumps cause my knee kepted stickin. Gil was almost the best at it. He went for like one-fifty. But this other kid called Footy almost hit two hunnert.

Did they let him go back to the Shelf?

Shooo. Shelf, *nothin*. The only thing that happened to Footy was he disappeared.

You think they did somethin to him?

I'd bet my shoes they quickdusted his ass. Them Syndicate jokers was always promisin somethin. If we cut into a wall this deep we'd get orange sodapop. If we split this much rock we'd get chocolate ice cream. If we stayed quiet they'd let us talk later. But didn't none of it never happen. You'd start tastin that orange sodapop like it was fizzin right down your throat. Feelin that ice cream all smooth and chocolatey in your belly. Thinkin of all the stuff you wanted to tell someone. Start imaginin your own voice in your head. It would drive you like three ways of crazy, G. They just wanted to see how far they could get us to go. And then whoever could go the farthest or was the best at somethin would wind up like that kid Footy.

Wind up missin.

Missin or croaked, G.

Was you good friends, you and Gil?

He was my best bud, galldangitall. Kid could hide bettern anyone. Sang this song all the time, too. The Chocolate London Song or something like that.

I was like, Chocolate *Funfun* Song. His big brother sings it, too.

Gil was always tryin to make everyone feel better. We talked about shaggin up outta the Pits together. We had it all planned and everything. But then he didn't wake up that mornin and this big bastard with a shovel came and scooped him into one of them bodyboxes. Scooped him up like he was a *dog* or a *bird*, not no *kid*. That was about the worst thing I ever seen. Can't stand shovels no more. Picks nuther.

Then we didn't say nothing for a while. He started trying to pull the snaps off his Syndicate slacks. They wouldn't budge none but he tried anyway. That was the first time I really looked at Oakley Brownhouse. I thought he might look kind of handsome if he got cleaned and combed his hair. Not handsome in no *Inch Bluestroke* way but handsome in a *little* way, the same way dogs and fish can be handsome if you stare at them long enough. He had these big brown eyes that looked nice in the candlelight. Even though he was all skinny and ratty and he had all them blisters and scratches on his chest he wasn't too bad.

I thought about kissing him for a minute but I didn't. I figured his mouth would taste like beans and franks and who knows what else.

If you're going to kiss a boy you better not think about it too much. You got to just do it and get it over with. I kissed Shale Bluehouse once when he didn't expect it. I don't even know why I did it. I think it's cause he was just sitting all sad and quiet and the way the light was crawling up the side of his face looked nice, like his face was kind of *glowing* or something.

Instead of kissing Oakley Brownhouse I kind of reached out and touched his face. I was like, Sorry I hit you before. I get wild sometimes.

He went, You better keep that nonsense under *control*, G.

I took my hand back.

You're lucky I don't hit *you*.

Then there was some more silence. You could hear the rain getting angry and you could hear the Bone Trees creaking and you could hear Honeycut singing in the back of the life hole. His voice was all small like it was a gazillion miles away.

Oakley Brownhouse pointed at my privacy and went, What's wrong with you?

I was like, Ain't nothin wrong with me.

You been clutchin your cooterfish like it's gonna run away and jump in the river.

I was like, It's just a little blood, Skinnybones.

You don't put nothin up in it?

I was like, Am I spose to?

Down in the Pits they was stuffin rags up in themselves.

I went, What kinda rags?

Old newspapers. Crappinslips. Parts of their clothes. Whatever they could find that was clean. There wasn't many of them bleedy girls. Maybe five or six. They was lucky cause the Syndicate didn't put em on the Black Bus. You know what they do to you on the Black Bus? About that doctor?

I heard about it.

Syndicate don't even know some of them girls is down there. Always hidin the blood in their pants.

Oakley Brownhouse started scratching his chest again. I could see him staring at the cans of beans and franks we ate. He was staring at them with his mouth open and he was staring so hard it was like he thought he could imagine the food back in the cans and go over and eat it again.

For some reason I went, I got a friend down in the Pits.

Oakley Brownhouse was like, I'll bet *every* galldangin body's got a friend down there, G.

I just nodded.

Every galldangin body there is.

I should be down there with him.

He was like, Yeah?

I went, Yeah.

Then he picked another scab off of his digits and said, Well, I don't wanna talk about it no more.

Okay.

I don't never wanna talk about it again.

• • •

There was a ditch dog outside. At first I thought it was a Undertwelve crying. Oakley Brownhouse had his head all pressed up against the front of the life hole and he was going, You hear that, G? You hear that?

I pressed my ear to the front and it sounded like the scaredest, smallest dog I ever heard. I started to open the door, but Oakley Brownhouse practically kicked me.

What is you *doin*, G!

Then I heard it again and I pushed Oakley Brownhouse aside and opened the life hole.

The rain was coming down so hard it looked like it was raining *up*, like the Shelf was sending it back toward the Creature Clouds so it would have more just in case it runned out.

About twenty feet in front of the life hole there was this little ditch dog. It was crying and limping and its muzzlestrap was tied all tight around its snout. One of its back legs was twisted funny like God made it that way. Just looking at it made you sad. Even though it was a ditch dog it still made you sad.

I started walking toward it. I thought maybe I would give it some washed water or a can of beans and franks or something. I walked slow and careful and I kept my hand over my eyes so I could see through the rain. When I got about ten feet away, Oakley Brownhouse came running from behind. He runned from behind and he runned at the dog like nothing I never seen before. He runned so fast and angry it was like *he* was a dog, too. Like he grew fangs and a tail and was going to start barking right there. But he didn't start barking and he didn't change into no dog. Instead, Oakley Brownhouse started *kicking* that ditch dog. He started kicking it and crying out and he was crying so loud you couldn't even hear the words under the crying. I couldn't watch it cause I kept thinking about that ditch dog's poor crooked leg. So I just sat down. I sat down right in the rain and I covered my eyes. All you could hear was the sound of Oakley Brownhouse's feet blasting into the ditch dog. I hated him when I heard that. I hated him more than I ever hated anything in my life.

Something *made* Oakley Brownhouse that way. Somehow I knowed that. It was something in the rain or something in the Creature Clouds or something that stayed with him from the Pits.

I sat in the rain and waited for Oakley Brownhouse to finish.

A few minutes later he came back covered with mud and his shoulders was all scratched and bleedy-looking.

He wiped some mud off his mouth and went, Galldangin thing got away. If I coulda got one more kick in. Just one more . . .

When we went back inside he begged me for another can of beans and franks but I wouldn't give it to him.

We didn't say nothing for the rest of the night.

SUPERBEANS AND SUPERFRANKS

To stay warm I sleep in the greatcoat.

At night the cold creeps in Honeycut's life hole like a big frozen hand.

Honeycut sleeps next to me and he don't cover himself with nothing cause he says he don't get cold. I think it's cause of how big he is. It's like his blobbiness is a extra set of *clothes* or something. He sleeps on his back and for some reason he's always got to touch me with his finger. If he ain't touching me he'll start huffing and crying like I disappeared or something. It's funny cause it don't matter *where* he touches me, as long as it's *part* of me. Even if it's the bottom of my *shoe* it's okay.

Oakley Brownhouse don't never sleep and he's always pacing around and talking to himself all nervous and jittery.

The first night he stayed with us I was like, Ain't you tired, Oakley Brownhouse?

He was like, Hells yeah I'm tired, G.

You look burnt.

You look burnt.

I patted the greatcoat. Lay down, boy. Get some sleep.

Don't feel like it.

You sick?

I ain't sick.

Scared?

Ain't scared, nuther.

You got gas or somethin?

I don't got gas, G. I just don't feel like sleepin, okay?

On his third night in the life hole, he told me how the Syndicate soldiers take turns doing wake-up shifts and how they carry pokersticks and nudge you in the ribs if they catch you sleeping. He said that some of them even got electricity sticks and that when you get nudged with one of them it feels like a bunch of giant *bees* stinging you. He said that the first time he got the electricity stick his body shut down and he just sat there all still and numb and had to wait for his legs to start working again. And he said that after the second or third time you get stuck your arm might just start flopping on its own.

I didn't mess with him no more about sleeping after that.

Sometimes I'll catch him trying to open a can of beans and franks, too. I'll be peeking through my lidslits and I'll see him snooping in the food trunk and trying to bust through the top of the can with the belt buckle, but he ain't strong enough. It's kind of funny cause he's always looking over his shoulder all scared and frantic like he's robbing a *bank* or something.

I'm like, Who's out to get you, Oakley Brownhouse?

He's like, What?

Then I'll say, Little lost outlaw boy.

And he'll go, Shut up, G!

My other favorite thing about Oakley Brownhouse is that when he makes his dooks he's always shouting at you to turn away. We don't got no slop closet, so unless you're in the back room, you can't help but see him squatting over the bucket and twisting his face all scrunchnosed like some kind of starved and electrocuted bushchicken. I try to not-look, but you can't really help it.

He's always like, Don't *look*!

And I'm like, I ain't lookin!

Yes you is!

No I ain't!

Go in the other *room*, G!

Honeycut's in there. Ain't no space.

Then go outside!

Go outside and do *what*?

I don't know. Stick a stick up your butt!

Stick a stick up *you*, Spazzboy!

Ditchbreath!

Ratface!

Hookerhead!

Chickendick!

One thing we need is a extra slop bucket. I know that sounds gross, but it's true. Too many dooks will make you want to go live in a sodabush for a while. Too many dooks will make you want to jump right in the Red River.

Hey, G.

Hey, Oakley Brownhouse.

Lemme ask you somethin.

Go head.

Why you got two differnt color eyes?

I don't know.

You a witch or somethin?

A *witch*?

Yeah, G. Hocus pocus try and joke us.

I'll hocus pocus *you*.

I can't even look at em.

Why not?

It's like lookin at a *shark* or somethin.

A shark!

A shark or a boogywolf. Or some freaky thing you find in a compost bin.

A compost bin!

I'm just bein honest, G.

I like my eyes. Just cause yours is so plain and muddy.

My eyes ain't muddy!

Muddy like the Red River . . . Bet I can stare at somethin longer than you.

Bet you can't, G.

How much?

You don't got no money.

How many pinches?

I ain't bettin *pinches*.

You gotta bet somethin, G.

That messed him up, calling him G. He couldn't even answer so I went, How bout kisses?

Huh?

How many kisses you bet me, Oakley Brownhouse?

I ain't bettin no galldangin *kisses*!

You must not got too strong a stare.

Strongern yours.

Then bet me some kisses.

No way. Totally grosses me out.

I was like, Then you lose. Ha ha.

Ha ha nothin.

Ha ha *ha*.

Ha ha *double* nothin, G.

You lose, Oakley Brownhouse.

THE NIGHT THE MOON CAME DOWN

Honeycut spends most of his time building the elephant. When you're in the front of the life hole all you can hear is how he tries to talk to it.

He's like, We gonna find him, ain't we, Elton? We gonna find Gil. And then you'll hear a pause, like he's listening to Elton, and after that pause you'll hear something like, I know, I *know*, Elton, like they're having a real conversation.

One night after I cleaned up and showed Oakley Brownhouse how to wash his own water, I went in there to give Honeycut a can of beans and franks, cause sometimes Honeycut goes so honking ballistic about building Elton that he forgets to *eat*.

You couldn't see too good cause most of the candles was burnt down to nubs. The few candles that was still going was flaming their little flames and you could see them dancing silver on the side of the elephant.

Elton the Elephant was almost finished. He was as tall as Honeycut and he had this long crooked trunk and one big floppy ear that looked more like this barber's ear who used to cut our hair at the Holy Family Agency. That barber was called Skinny Dave and both his ears was all long and stretched out like they got pulled real hard or something.

I was surprised that Elton looked like a elephant. I imagined that he would look more like a *bear* or some kind of *dinosaur* or even a *ice cream truck* before all the ice cream trucks was turnt into Syndicate rigs.

To tell you the truth, I ain't never seen no real elephant. I only seen pictures of them when I was at the Holy Family Agency. Me and Shale used to look at this one book that had all these photographs of wild animals from this place called Africa. I remember this one Bluehouse Sister with no chin tried to tell us that elephants was like these holy creatures cause they live for like a gazillion years and when they croak all the other elephants carry the bones of the croaked elephants back to a big elephant graveyard where they have this big honking party. I thought that sounded kind of crazy, especially cause of the way that Sister told us, with her eyes all big and spooky-looking and her chin all smashed and missing. Shale Bluehouse was afraid of that Sister and he always called her Sister Nochin.

I stood there while Honeycut worked on one of the back legs. His face was all serious and didn't have no real expression and his forehead was all knotted up and he was kind of biting his lower lip.

I was like, Hey, Honeycut.

He looked up and smiled and when he smiled it was like someone was tickling him with a big invisible feather.

He was like, Toof Fanny come yet?

I went, Not yet. But she will.

Tell Honey when she come okay, Winsdy?

You'll be the first to know, Honeycut, I promise.

I walked over to him and handed him the beans and franks and he stood there and ate the whole can with his big finger in about thirty seconds.

I went, How's it goin?

Honeycut sucked the last beanbits off his finger and went, Honey maked Elton's *ears*. He touched the first ear and then he grabbed a bigger aluminum blob and smoothed it with his hands and shaped and flattened it and went to the other side of the head and attached it and just like that he made the other ear. It was funny how he tried to make them look *human*.

Sister Nochin also told me and Shale Bluehouse how elephants can hear things that are like a gazillion miles away cause of how big the drums in their ears is. She said they can hear hummingbirds crying and puppies laughing on the other side of the world and stuff like that.

Honeycut touched the ears and was like, Gil's supersmall so you gotta listen real *good*.

I bet Elton'll hear him.

I said that and I don't know why I did. I wanted to tell Honeycut how Gil was dead and all, right there. I wish I would have, but I couldn't.

Instead I was like, You should make a tail.

He went, A *tail!?*

Yeah. A tail. I think elephants got tails. It's like their radar.

Raydar?

Yeah. Like a radio stick.

Mean Bob had a radio. He putted it on Honey's head and maked it *buzz!*

I went, Their tail helps them keep their ears tuned in.

That stuff about radar and the radio stick got Honeycut all excited. He handed me the empty can of beans and turnt and bent down and grabbed a blob of aluminum and started making this crazy-looking tail. It was kind of funny cause it definitely wasn't no elephant tail. It looked more like a *beaver's* tail and when he stuck it on the elephant's big silver butt it looked like some kind of crooked *paddle* that was going to make it *swim* or something.

Elton the Elephant was finished.

Honeycut circled Elton a few times and then stopped by his trunk and kind of bent down and listened. He put his ear real close to this slot that looked like the elephant's mouth.

After he listened for a minute, Honeycut stepped back and smiled his big oafy blobsmile and started laughing.

I was like, What's so funny?

Honeycut looked at me and said, Elton just tolted me about the Moon.

The Moon?

Yuh-huh.

What about the Moon?

It's comin down tonight.

That was the night the jellyfishes stopped swimming out of me.

It's funny how the body does stuff like that to you. One minute it wants to make a bunch of jellyfishes blob out of your privacy and you think the world is going to end, and then the next minute that ballistickness just sort of goes away like some dust dusting in the wind and you realize that the jellyfishes ain't swimming down no more and just like that your privacy is doing okay again.

I guess those is the kinds of things you got to deal with as a woman. Even if you ain't really no *grown* woman yet, there's still all that stuff that the body does to you, like putting stones in your boobies and making you feel all hot and squishy.

I watched Oakley Brownhouse a lot that night. I wasn't watching him the way you watch a ditch dog snuffling in a compost bin and I wasn't watching him the way you watch birds when there was still birds flying around to watch. I was watching him the way you watch something you want to *eat*. I ain't saying that I wanted to *eat* Oakley Brownhouse or nothing gross like that—I ain't saying that at all. It was just sort of this *hungry* feeling I had, and that hungry feeling was in my stomach and in my hands and it was kind of tingling where those stones in my boobies was pressing.

At first I thought that that hungry feeling was there cause of what Second Staff Brown done to me in the sodabush. I thought maybe he put something inside me that would always make that hungry feeling come. I still ain't sure if that was part of it or not. All I know is that I was looking at little Oakley Brownhouse with his 437 on his arm, and I could feel the blood bleeding through my heartmuscles and the bones moving all slow and eager under my skin.

Honeycut was in the back, putting the finishing touches on Elton the Elephant. You could hear him singing the Chocolate Funfun Song.

I stacked all the cans and scraped the waxblobs off the floor and tried to clean up a little.

Oakley Brownhouse was pacing around the life hole and hugging his little bony shoulders and kind of looking behind him all ballistic and spookfaced, so I stepped in front of him and I went, Let's go for a walk.

He was like, A *walk*?

Yeah, a walk.

He went, What is you, *crazy*? and tried to walk around me but I cut him off.

Sissychicken.

Sissychicken, my assbone!

I pushed him in the chest a little and went, We'll go look at the Red River, Oakley Brownhouse. Stare at the Creature Clouds. Come on. No one'll see us.

He kind of patted at his little dinky chest where I pushed him and went, You wanna get *clinched*? What about the ditch dogs, G?

You can hear em comin.

Get that ass bit up, too. Bit up and sent down to the Pits.

We'll be real careful.

He went, Them Syndicate jokers is walkin around with *torches*, and he said it like his head was going to pop off or something.

I was like, If they got torches it'll be easy to see em comin. Let's go.

He paced all fast and crazy for a minute and kind of muttered to himself and then stopped real fast and went, We get clinched I'ma smack you right in your titties.

I was like, Oh, *please*, and I pushed him in the chest again.

So we smeared ourselves with Second Staff Brown's safe jam. I tried to smear some on Oakley Brownhouse, but he just waved my hand away and did it himself. It was funny how Oakley Brownhouse turnt all white and sticky from the safe jam. Just when you think a Digit Kid can't get no whiter, go and smear some safe jam on him, I swear. He looked like he crawled out of a giant carton of *milk*.

Oakley Brownhouse was like, This stuff *stinks*, G.

I was like, It stinks cause it works.

I told Honeycut we'd be back and he oafed and yuh-huhed and said something to Elton the Elephant and acted like Elton the Elephant was saying something back to him, and then me and Oakley Brownhouse ducked through the front of the life hole and out into the night.

The rain was almost sideways and the Bone Trees was bending and you could hear the wind whistling through the branches. It sounded like a little train full of screaming cats and it was like that cat train was a gazillion miles away.

We walked real slow and careful so we wouldn't make too much noise. Oakley Brownhouse was singing this little coward song through his nose. I kept telling him that I would protect him, but he just kept rubbing his hands together all frantic and skittery, saying that no *girl* could protect him—especially no Under*twelve* girl that ain't never been down to the *Pits*—and he kept singing that song through his little pale milk nose.

There was a funny metal color boiling in the Creature Clouds. They wasn't all black and gray and bruised-looking like usual. That night they had this almost *blue* color climbing up their bellies. And they was making the Bone Trees glow kind of blue and gray and this other color that ain't even been invented yet.

As we got closer to the other side of the Bone Trees, you could hear this murmuring. There was like a gazillion voices, and they was all hushed and secret-sounding. You could feel the heat in the voices but it didn't seem like there was words. It was more like the voices was *wind* or *rain* or something.

After a few more steps you could tell that those voices was coming from down by the Red River. Oakley Brownhouse tried to turn and run, but I grabbed his arm real quick and told him to stop being a sissychicken. He swallowed this big glurp in his throat and kind of stuttered a few more parts of his nose song and kept walking.

When we got to the edge of the Bone Trees, there was a gazillion Lost Men gathered at the edge of the Red River. Some of them was holding fire lanterns and some of them had old newspapers rolled up with flames flickering off the tops. All the lanterns and newspaperflames looked like a bunch of fireflies hovering at the banks.

At first I thought maybe the Lost Men was trying to rally together and organize some kind of big honking war with the Syndicate.

Tick Burrowman used to talk about how he would pull out this old blastergun that he kept in a shoebox if the Lost Men made a war with Astan Loe and the Syndicate. He said that he only had five bullets but he would save at least three of them for Astan Loe. He never showed me that blastergun, but I believed him just cause of the way his voice would go all scared and wavery when he talked about it.

I thought there was something funny like that going on, but there wasn't no fishflies jumping and I couldn't see the Salt Man nowhere and there wasn't nobody holding no blasterguns over their heads.

I thought I heard someone creeping up behind us, so I pulled Oakley Brownhouse into a sodabush. I pulled him hard and tight and I made him lay low.

After the creeping sound faded off toward the water, I bent the sodabush branches so we could see what was going on.

When you looked real close you could see how a bunch of Lost Men was kneeling right in the shallow part of the Red River and how their hands was clasped like they was *praying*. That murmuring was all low and hot and confused.

Their hands was clasped and they was all looking up at the Creature Clouds the way you're supposed to look at *God* or *Jesus* or a *holy tree* or something. When I looked up to see what they was seeing, I couldn't believe it.

It was the Moon.

There was this big long crack in the Creature Clouds and the Moon was just hanging there like a big swollen whale's heart. It was like the Creature Clouds had this incredible thought and the thought got so honking big it turnt into the Moon and just busted right through their bellies.

You could see the caves in its face and you could see how it was kind of whiter around the edges like there was something huge and bright burning behind it. All you could do was just stand there all dumb and spookfaced.

Oakley Brownhouse couldn't see it cause his eyes was closed and he was holding his fists over them like we was trapped in a cave with a bunch of vampire bats. I nudged him and called him King of the Sissychickens and then I pinched him and told him to open his eyes.

When he finally opened his eyes all the Lost Men was down on their knees in the water. They was all kind of praying and some of them was crying and me and Oakley just stood there all flatfaced and stunned.

You could see the reflection of the Moon kind of fluttering on the skin of the Red River. For some reason it made the water look all silver and clean.

Oakley Brownhouse was like, Galldangitall, G!

Then I said it, too. I went, Galldangitall, Oakley Brownhouse!

He went, It's the fuckin Moon!

I said it, too. I was like, It's the fuckin Moon!

When I looked at Oakley Brownhouse I could see the reflection of the Moon burning cold in his eye.

That's when I finally kissed him.

It made a sad little plopping sound like a pennycopper falling in a mudpuddle. It didn't feel like nothing special and we kind of bumped noses and knocked our teeth together. It felt more like something you do with a ham *sand*wich than a kiss, but it was still a kiss.

Oakley Brownhouse stared at me like he could see the Moon burning cold in my eye, too.

He was like, Damn, G.

And I was like, Damn, G.

Then I made him do it again and it felt like we was falling backwards through the bellies of the Creature Clouds. Like we was passing right over the face of that big old lost Moon.

Then the next thing I know, Oakley Brownhouse is kind of wiggling and squirming and he's singing that coward song through his nose.

I tried to grab him but he was too fast. I reached out again but he had already turnt and squeezed through the branches of the sodabush. He slipped and fell and scrambled to his feet and when he stood up there was all this mud slimed in his hair and he looked like some kind of miniature Lost Man who left his brain in a compost bin.

I went, Oakley Brownhouse, where you goin?!

He didn't say nothing and just started running wild.

I would have went after him, but I was too froze. My mouth was hot and my eyes felt huge and there was something tingling in the smallest parts of my bones.

I think that little Moon I seen burning cold in Oakley Brownhouse's eye was making that feeling.

I think that little Moon was the most handsomest thing I ever seen.

THE HUNDREDTH DOUBLEDAY
OF RAIN

It was the hundredth doubleday of rain and I had fallen for a little Undertwelve Digit Kid called Oakley Brownhouse.

I dripped a waxblob on the floor and scratched in a One and two Zeros. And I scratched a little heart next to it so I would always know the number.

It was the hundredth doubleday of rain and everything felt new like there was little lovefeathers tickling the muscles in my heart.

I wanted to climb to the top of the Shelf and take Slocumb Yardly's bullhorn and tell the whole big honking lost world. I wanted my voice to fly right over the Bone Trees and over the Red River and over the Forsaken Lawn. I wanted my lovevoice to fly all the way to Toptown.

On the hundredth doubleday of rain Oakley Brownhouse finally slipped off to sleep. I think he forgot about those Syndicate soldiers and their pokersticks. I think he forgot about being all ballistic and nervous. You can only pace and fidget and scratch the digits on your shoulder for so long before you just get tired.

He was all curled up in the corner like a little alleycat when there was still alleycats that curled in corners. His face was all quiet and pale and you could see the flames from the candles glowing soft on the muscles over his eyes and when you bent real close you could see these tiny blue bloodveins in the skin of his lids like pretty little spider feet.

I watched his eyes flutter and I listened to his breath slooshing in and out of his lungbags, and then I kind of laid down and curled my body right around him. At first he didn't even feel me and just kept sleeping. That's the first time I smelled him. Even though none of us ain't had no bath since we all got together, Oakley Brownhouse had this little smell that made my knees feel like they was made out of *chocolate ice cream.* Like they was made out of chocolate ice cream *and* they was melting all over the place. It wasn't even a smell you can describe, like butter or cheese or burning leaves. It was something else. It wasn't no mansmell and it wasn't no womansmell. I guess it was a Oakley Brownhouse *boy*smell. Like something you smell when you walk into a room where there's some nice furniture and a fireplace or something. And maybe there's something burning in that fireplace that makes you feel kind of warm and slippery inside. I know that don't make no sense, but that's kind of what his smell was like. I had to snuffle right near his underarms to get the whole thing, which sounds kind of gross, but that's what I did. I curled around his little body and snuffled right up to his armpit.

So on the hundredth doubleday of rain—the night after the Moon came down—I was snuffling into Oakley Brownhouse and feeling all warm and slippery when he kind of turnt and spun.

He went, *Hey!* and pushed away from me and stood real fast. He kind of started walking this little circle around the room.

What the heck you *doin*, G? Tryin to *pickpocket* me and shit?

I just sat there and watched him try to pull the snaps off his Syndicate slacks. He wasn't never going to pull them snaps off but he kept trying.

He stopped after a minute and was like, I prolly got *bugs* from you, and started clawing at his digits.

That night I made Oakley Brownhouse sleep with me on the greatcoat. I tried to get him to roll in close but he wouldn't. He kept saying that it made him itch, and he kept calling me G and kind of pushing my hands away like they was monkeyhands or something. I didn't care cause those feathers was still tickling the muscles in my heart and those stones in my boobies was all tingly and warm-feeling.

I dreamed that me and Oakley Brownhouse was in a wedding with a big metal band. I dreamed that there was a bunch of Digit Kids all lined up and you could see the numbers on their arms and you could see the quickdust smears scuffed on their shoes and how their heads was shaved, too.

And even though those Digit Kids was all quickdust-smeared and bald, they was all smiling and happy and singing this love song that was kind of like Honeycut's Chocolate

Funfun Song except the words was different. They was about me and Oakley Brownhouse, not the chickenhouse or the pickleshack or all those other things Honeycut sings about.

During the love song, all the Digit Kids was kind of joining hands and swaying in their Numbering Line. There was some Undertwelves who wasn't Digit Kids yet and they was right there holding hands, too. When it was through, Mosely Minifield touched our foreheads and told me and Oakley Brownhouse that we was *boy and wife* and told us we could kiss and we tonguekissed in front of all the Digit Kids and licked each other's teeth and everyone went all ballistic and the shouts flew through the sliding rain and over the Shelf and they busted right through the Creature Clouds and flew into outer space for a gazillion miles.

DOUBLE VANISHING

I t was cold in the life hole and my breath was smoking.

The last thing I remember was his body next to me all twisted into itself. The greatcoat was gone and my ribs hurt from sleeping on the floor.

I went into the back room. The candles was pinched and there wasn't no Honeycut and Elton the Elephant was gone too. All that was left was a few scraps of aluminum smashed in the corners like little metal fish.

I couldn't remember the last time I seen Honeycut. It might have been a full doubleday. It might have been a halfweek. I knowed it had something to do with the Moon coming down, but everything was all blurry cause of how my heart was aching for Oakley Brownhouse. It felt all strange and heavy like it was turning into a *goat's* heart. And there's nothing more ballistic-feeling than having a *goat's* heart beating in your chest.

I knowed I would have to go looking for Honeycut cause the muscles in his brain was too little for him to be safe by himself. I figured he'd probably wind up back in the Red River with the Salt Man and the voodoo fishes.

For some reason I started pretending Oakley Brownhouse was still in the life hole.

When I started to leave he went, *Where you goin, G?*

I was like, *I gotta find Honeycut.*

Lemme go with you!

But I just pretended like I couldn't hear him and smeared some safe jam on my arms and face and slipped into Tick Burrowman's garbage bag.

Before I left I went, *Don't go nowhere. I'll be right back.*

He was like, *Cool, G. I ain't goin nowhere.*

I pushed on through the front of Honeycut's life hole and headed out into the sliding rain.

The wind was weak and the Bone Trees looked like they was resting, but the rain was still falling and I was glad that it wasn't going sideways cause I could see without getting too much of it in my eyes.

I figured Honeycut would have Elton the Elephant with him and they would both be real easy to spot, partly cause of the elephant being all silver and partly cause both of them is so honking *big*.

There was some Syndicate soldiers patrolling the rim of the Shelf. Some had electricity sticks and some had blaster-guns propped on their shoulders. I stayed at the edge of the Bone Trees so I could hide behind a treetrunk or dive into a sodabush. For some reason I kept talking to Oakley Brownhouse even though he wasn't there. I was like, *Keep quiet* and *Don't be a sissychicken!*

It looked like those Syndicate soldiers was put there so couldn't nobody could come climbing up out of the Pits. Two of them appeared over the rim and then three more. Then there was a group of three ditch dogs with their snouts all muzzlestrapped.

I turnt and started running back through the Bone Trees. I thought Honeycut might have headed toward the Red River. The rain had picked up a little and I had to run with my hand over my eyes.

Between these two Bone Trees I could see someone. It wasn't no Syndicate soldier and it wasn't no Lost Man. When I got closer I could see that whatever it was was wearing this long hooded cloak. I stopped and it stopped and then the person swept the hood back. It was that Babymaker woman who was in Tick Burrowman's life hole that one night. I could tell it was her cause of how blue her eyes was. They was so blue you could almost *taste* them. She was so pale and pretty she looked like some kind of statue. She reached into her pocket and throwed something to me. It was small and dark and round. After I catched it I started toward her but I seen some torches torching through the Bone Trees. They was somersaulting all ballistic and zigzaggy and you could hear feet running and things sliding on the ground.

When I looked back, the Babymaker woman was gone. I walked over to where she was standing and I looked around but I didn't see nothing. I opened my hand.

I was holding a plum.

It was hard and cold and so purple it looked black. I could almost taste it through my hand.

I searched for the Babymaker woman again but I couldn't find her so I headed back to the life hole. I squeezed the plum in my hand cause it felt like it would keep me from being scared.

I was getting real tired and I started to think of all the things I would tell Honeycut if I finded him. I would tell him how I wasn't thirty-three years old and about how Tick Burrowman was trying to sell me to the woman with the long black car and I would tell him about the jellyfishes and I would tell him about Gil, too. I would tell him cause you can't just go around protecting kids like Honeycut from the truth.

All that thinking made me ache inside. I was aching the way the Creature Clouds must ache cause of all the poison in their bellies.

Even though he wasn't there, I was like, *Stop cryin, Oakley Brownhouse! Stop actin like a little girl!*

That's when I finally seen Honeycut. He was sitting right in the middle of a Bone Tree that was like a gazillion feet tall. It was probably the most ballistic Bone Tree in all the Bone Trees cause its branches was twisted funny and looked like some old hairy chicken legs.

Way at the top you could see Elton the Elephant. He was so high up it looked like a little lost Christmas ornament. Like the wind blew it there all the way from Toptown or something.

I shouted up to him. I was like, Hey, Honeycut!

I could hear Honeycut kind of oafing and crying but he didn't hear me so I shouted up to him again.

I went, Hey, Honeycut! Honeycut Greenhouse!

But he still couldn't hear me cause of the rain and the wind.

Then I waited for the wind to croak a little and I went, Hey, Honeycut Greenhouse, you big honking baby, sing the Chocolate Funfun Song!

He looked down, and even though he was like a gazillion feet high in that tree, I could still see his big forehead and how it was all twisted up from crying.

What is you *doin*, Winsdy?

I'm lookin for you, Dorkboy! What are *you* doin?

Honeycut went, Honey and Elton is lookin for *Gil*.

I was like, Well, you ain't gonna find him up there!

Yes I is! We's gonna find him, ain't we, Elton!?

Come down, Honeycut!

He went, Nuh-uh.

The Syndicate's all over the Shelf. Ditch dogs is everywhere. You wanna get clinched?

Honeycut was like, Honey ain't comin down till he finds his bruddah.

. . . What if you gotta go to the bathroom?

Honey don't care.

You're just gonna go in your pants?

Winsdy's mean!

That's when I said it. I went, He's *dead*, Honeycut!

Honeycut stuck his big blobfinger right in his mouth like he didn't hear me so I said it again.

I went, Gil's *dead*!

Honeycut kind of scrunched his forehead up and said, His name ain't *Fred*.

Dead, I said. I said he's *dead*.

Gil ain't dead.

Yes he is, Honeycut. Oakley Brownhouse knowed him in the Pits. They was best friends. It's true!

Honey don't believe Winsdy!

I didn't even wanna *tell*ya, okay?

Winsdy's mean! Winsdy's meaner than Mean Bob!

I was like, Whensday's tellin you the *truth*, Honeycut! And Honeycut needs to get down outta that tree before he gets *clinched*!

Then all you could hear through the sliding rain and the whistling wind was Honeycut's crying. It was the biggest crying I ever heard, and I knowed those Syndicate soldiers over at the Shelf rim would hear it and come running.

I held the plum up and went, The Tooth Fairy came!

He was like, She did?

Yep. See? I turned the plum between my fingers.

. . . What is it?

It's a plum.

That's from the Toof Fanny?

She said you was so good you might get two.

His face went ballistic and he tried to reach his hand out like he'd be able to touch the plum.

That's when the ditch dogs started coming. Their barks was small and far away, but their muzzlestraps was off now and you just knowed they'd be there any minute. It's like the noise of the barks get louder and louder and just turn into the *dogs*. Then the Syndicate voices started coming, too. The voices *and* the barks.

I had to go cause I would have got clinched.

For some reason while I was running back to Honeycut's life hole I started looking for the Moon. I looked and looked and looked, but there wasn't nothing to see but the rain going sideways and the tops of the Bone Trees bending ugly and those old swollen bellies in the Creature Clouds hanging dark and angry.

I knowed there would be trouble. I could feel it sliding through me.

When I got back to Honeycut's life hole, my legs was all swollen and heavy and I was wet and tired and my ankles was all cut and itchy. After I slowed my breath and drinked some washed water out of one of the beans and franks cans, I sat down and wiped the blood and dirt off my face and ankles.

Part of me was glad cause I got away from the Syndicate and

the ditch dogs, but part of me was real worried and frantic cause I knowed something bad was going to happen to Honeycut.

For some reason I started looking for Oakley Brownhouse. He wasn't over by the slop bucket and he wasn't behind the foodlocker neither. You could *feel* how Oakley Brownhouse wasn't in the life hole and that feeling was like having a big bone pulled out of your body, like one of those superbones that keeps your leg muscles strong so you can run.

My hands started shaking and my heart felt like it had a big black bruise on it. I needed Oakley Brownhouse the way you need food or washed water. I felt sick and that sickness was like something small and hot and hungry running in my stomach.

That's when I started to cry. I cried like I ain't never cried in my life. I didn't even recognize the noises my mouth and throat was making. It was like those noises was being made by some kind of *machine* that I couldn't see.

I started walking this circle around Honeycut's life hole. It was the biggest circle I could make. At first I walked slow, but then I started going faster and faster like there was a motor inside me, like whatever that machine was that was making those crying noises was making me walk all crazy and ballistic, too. It felt like if I could walk enough circles, things would get better somehow, like Oakley Brownhouse would come back and Honeycut would be in his aluminum room with Elton the Elephant. I know that don't make no sense, but that's how it felt, so I just kept doing it. I walked faster and faster around the life hole, crying my big dumb honking sissychicken tears.

I started talking to Oakley Brownhouse again. I was like, *We gotta get some plastic for you, Oakley Brownhouse. We gotta get some plastic . . .*

I kept saying that over and over till I got tired and just sat on the floor. I sat for a long time. I felt so lonesome I thought I was disappearing. I kept looking at my hands to make sure they was still there. The fingers was all there and it still felt like there was bones in my wrists. The same kind of bones that birds got. *Bones and fingers,* I kept telling myself. *Bones and fingers . . .*

After a while I decided to go back and see if Honeycut was okay. I didn't care if they clinched me no more.

I walked and it felt like my legs was just moving on their own. Like my nerves and my muscles and the parts that connect your bones to the muscles in your brain was all numb and small and bored.

Bones and fingers, I kept telling myself. *Bones and fingers and legs. Keep the blood in your heart, Whensday. Don't let it turn into no goat's heart . . .*

The rain didn't really matter. And I was hungry, too. But my hunger was small and hot like a spider crawling in your stomach. I fell down and got back up and kept walking. I think I started walking sideways cause I kept bumping into Bone

Trees. But I kept moving cause I had this feeling that if I stopped for too long I wouldn't be able to go no further, like I would turn into a Bone Tree and some roots would bust through the floors in my shoes.

But when I got there there wasn't no Syndicate soldiers and there wasn't no ditch dogs and there wasn't no Honeycut. There wasn't nobody for what seemed like a gazillion miles. Nothing but big old hairy Bone Trees.

I was too late.

I was too late and the rain was going so ballistically sideways that it was like it was coming from the *Pits*.

For some reason I started eating my plum. It was cold and a little sour and when I swallowed it it felt like I was swallowing my own heart.

It seemed like everybody in the world had disappeared and the only people left was a girl called Whensday and a big funny-looking elephant on the top of that Bone Tree.

DREAM OF WORDS

Oh you big lost world you big lost world you big lost stupid world so lost and completely honking ballistic always raining raining raining raining down raining down like everything's falling falling falling like everything's always falling away falling away and above and outside and inside raining down raining down raining down all that poison falling how dare you bring the Creature Clouds how dare you bring them here how dare you bring the Creature Clouds to the Shelf with all their heat and fire and their groaning and their black bellies sagging like a big bag full of blood ready to bust and bleed and break that sagging if you had a leg I'd kick it I'd kick it I'd kick that leg I'd kick that leg I'd kick you right in the shins cause there ain't no reason for this there ain't no reason for this there ain't no honking reason cause it don't make no sense it don't make no sense and I could throw a rock at you I could throw two rocks at you and me and Shale Bluehouse could throw a gazillion billion Shelf rocks at you cause there ain't no sense no more there ain't no sense no more there ain't no sense in my hands or my legs or my privacy and the blood in my body and the blood in my hands and the blood in my privacy don't make no sense swimming out of me swimming out of me swimming out of me like the Red River all dead and spoiled and full of fishflies and voodoo fishes and maybe fishflies turn into voodoo fishes and maybe voodoo fishes turn into ditch dogs and maybe ditch dogs turn into Syndicate soldiers and God's always taking things away always taking things away he's always taking things cause that's all God does and God will just take and take and take everything and it's like God is clinching everything all the time and God is everything that he does and God is everything that is done and God is everything that don't get done and God is the world and God is a Bone Tree and God is a ditch dog and God is a thunderhorse and God is the Creature Clouds with their big swollen black bellies full of blood and God is the Syndicate and God is the Red River and God is a fishfly and God is a big honking ballistic thief with his long slow hand and if God had a shin I would kick I would kick it I would kick it I would kick it so hard he would double over and grab it with his big holy Godhand he would triple over and clutch his shinbone and some wild wind from the Pits would come flying out of his mouth and the wind would have a color and the color would be so honking ugly that it wouldn't have a name and that wind would blow up through the Shelf and make the walls cry in every life hole and that crying would be like a thousand kittens getting drowned in the Pits cause my kick would break his bone would break his bone would make his bone pop like a blastergun like a blastergun popping and if I had a blastergun I'd shoot God right in the shins I'd shoot him right in the shins I'd point it at his shins and pull the trigger and make that bone pop like a blastergun like a blastergun like a blastergun popping and if I had a blastergun I'd shoot God right in the shins and make that bone pop and maybe someone else would become God maybe someone else would become God maybe someone else would become God maybe someone else would grow a beard and get some miracle skills and take over the world like maybe someone who ain't in the Syndicate like someone who ain't from Toptown like someone who ain't friends with Astan Loe like someone who don't ride around on thunderhorses and clinch little kids like someone who don't drive big long black cars maybe someone . . .

III

THE BODYBOX BOAT

ou can hear the ditch dogs. You can't see them but you can hear them barking and you can imagine their teeth all sharp and yellow. Yellow like the Oldmonday mush with twice the stink. All sharp and yellow and ready to eat you. You can feel their barking and it's like there's a gazillion superbarks buzzing through the bones in your hands. And you can imagine all the things that's scrunched in their gums, like dooks and quickdust and the bones of all the croaked Digit Kids. And you imagine it so good it's like you can smell the barking.

I'm standing in front of Tick Burrowman's life hole and I'm shivering cause the rain went cold. There ain't nothing worst than standing and shivering in the cold when all you got is a old flimsy garbage bag and a little bit of safe jam slimed over you.

Every time a ditch dog barks, my hand jerks like there's something biting it.

Even though he ain't really there I keep telling Oakley Brownhouse to stay calm. I'm like, *Stay calm, Oakley Brownhouse. He'll open the door, just stay calm.*

Poor Oakley Brownhouse. Poor little lost Digit Kid.

I ain't sure why I'm here. Maybe it's cause I was so close and the rain's so thick it feels like it's burning through the safe jam.

Once Shale Bluehouse cried with no sound for two days after Murl Greenhouse and Spider Brownhouse stealed all his pennycoppers . . .

I just *know* he's going to open his door. I just *know*.

Now Shale keeps coat buttons in his frogpocket and sometimes he takes them out and kind of studies them like he's trying to figure out how to turn them into pennycoppers . . .

Come on, Tick Burrowman, open your door! Open your door open your door open your stupid honking door, Tick Burrowman!

The ditch dogs is on you like a fever . . .

I go, *Tick ain't gonna clinch us, Oakley Brownhouse. He don't got it in him.*

Maybe there's a couple of Syndicate soldiers sitting at his planing table. Maybe Tick Burrowman's showing off his new bodyboxes and giving them Oldmonday mush and cheese and everyone's drinking washed water and stomping their boots and laughing and talking about how big and fast their thunderhorses is.

Even though he ain't really there I make Oakley Brownhouse knock with me. Tick Burrowman'll see me all messed up and rain-burnt and he wouldn't try to hurt me or clinch me or sell me to some clown-faced woman in a big black car. Sell me like some furniture or something he made on his planing table.

So I knock and I knock and I knock till my knuckles hurt.

Shale Bluehouse can walk backwards better than he can walk forwards . . .

I pretend Oakley Brownhouse is shivering and sniffling next to me. I pretend so good it's like you can hear his *teeth*.

No one answers so I keep knocking.

If Shale would have showed the Syndicate how he could walk backwards, maybe . . .

The front of Tick Burrowman's life hole creaks open and this big honking *smell* blobs out. It ain't dooks and it ain't cheese and it ain't the Oldmonday mush gone bad. It's something else and I ain't never smelled nothing like it.

There ain't nobody standing in the entrance and all you can see is a few candles burning and a bunch of bodyboxes in the middle of the floor. The bodyboxes is all zigzagged and stacked funny. It almost looks like they're being turnt into something *else*.

There's this flap of plastic that's been nailed to the inside of the life hole now. I think maybe Tick Burrowman nailed it there cause the rain started leaking through.

A voice goes, Come in.

I kind of step in and push the flap aside but I don't close the front of the life hole. I got my hands scooped over my mouth and nose cause of the smell.

This is nasty, G.

Even though he ain't really there, I'm like, *I know I know I know, Oakley Brownhouse.*

191

Come in. Come in and close the hole.

That voice don't sound like Tick Burrowman's voice. It don't sound *nothing* like it.

I reach back and close the front of Tick Burrowman's life hole.

I look around and I see the entrance to the kitchencove and I see the sinkwell where we used to put the washed water and I see a bunch of doubleday rain numbers written all over the walls.

I'm like, That you, Tick Burrowman? I'm like, That you, old friend?

I listen but there's just the wind and the rain. And when there ain't no answer and all you hear is the wind and the rain it's like *super*wind and *super*rain.

I go, Tick Burrowman, if that's you, clap three times.

I wait but whoever it is won't come out and won't clap so I go, It's *me*. It's *Whensday* . . . Clap three times, Tick Burrowman. Just clap.

But there still ain't no claps. There still ain't no claps and all you can hear is that rain and that wind and how I'm not-breathing.

. . . Mister?

Let's get outta here, G!

I'm like, *Get outta here and go* where? To the voice I go, You a *mister*, ain't you?

Come on, G, Oakley Brownhouse says, and kind of stomps his foot.

I'm like, *Stop bein such a sissychicken!*

Then, all of the sudden, just when me and Oakley Brownhouse is about to start fighting about being and not-being sissychickens, the voice goes, Don't go.

I turn back to the bodyboxes, but you still can't see nobody. It's almost like the bodyboxes got a *voice*.

Please, the voice says again. Don't go.

I take another step into the room but you still can't see nothing. You can't see nothing but shadows crawling and numbers on the walls and flames flickering all slow and spooky.

Don't worry, the voice says. I ain't gonna hurt you. When he says *ain't* it sounds like he's getting poked or stabbed. Like he's about to start crying or something.

The smell is thicker now. It's thicker and hotter and I start to think that maybe the smell's been there all the time and I just didn't never notice it. Like maybe the muscles in my brain got used to it from living there all those halfweeks and mini-months.

The voice goes, You're a Undertwelve, ain't you.

I don't say nothing. I just sort of stand there with my hands over my mouth.

It's okay if you're a Undertwelve. Really, it's okay.

You can hear the wind and the rain and you can hear how the ditch dogs stopped barking.

The voice kind of goes wavery for a minute and says, If you're a Undertwelve I really ain't gonna do nothin . . .

Oakley Brownhouse is like, *Sure you ain't, B! Sure you ain't!*

. . . I ain't never clinched no one. Got any food?

I'm like, No.

Man, I could use some food. Some chicken.

I go, *Chicken*. There ain't no chickens no more.

Chicken and collyflowers.

Collyflowers?

Mmmmmm.

Collyflowers is gross.

I like em.

I'm like, Who are you?

Then the voice become a shadow and the shadow become hands and the hands become arms and the arms become a whole body and the whole body become a *big honking man* with spicy mansmells. You can smell him the way you can smell thunderhorses after they's been running. It's a smell I know from before, but it ain't Tick Burrowman's mansmell.

It's *Joe Painter* and he's all crouched and spookfaced behind a stack of bodyboxes and he's holding this winch that he uses for dragging trees. He's holding his winch and he's holding this homemade tool that looks like some kind of holepoker.

Joe Painter used to always walk into the life hole with that winch on his shoulder like he was *born* with it there, like if you knocked it off he would just start to *fade away* or something.

His arms is all full of sawdust and his face is filthy and there's all of these little purple spots covering his neck and shoulders. He's sweating so hard it looks like he's getting *cooked*.

I'm like, Hey, Joe Painter.

He goes, Hey, you, and just kind of stands there and stares at me. His eyes look huge and white like some eggs.

He goes, Ain't seen you around lately.

I'm like, I been around . . . Where's Tick Burrowman?

He went away.

I go, Away? and run into his little room. There ain't nothing in it but a couple of scattered dooks. It smells terrible.

Joe Painter goes, Syndicate got him. Flying Fox.

I run into the kitchencove. There ain't nothin in there neither.

When I come back out, Joe Painter goes, He went with the last group of Elders they found. Took him away with his hands over his head.

I try to picture that—Tick Burrowman being took away with his hands over his head—but the picture just makes me real tired. It makes me want to lay down right on the floor, so I stop.

I'm like, When'd that happen?

Joe Painter goes, After Second Staff Brown turnt up in the Red River.

He turnt *up*?

They dragged the riverbed when they was huntin the aluminum. Found Second Staff Brown instead. Said his head was twisted around. Twisted around like he saw somethin he shouldn'ta seen.

They think Tick Burrowman done it?

Had to blame someone.

He didn't do it, Joe Painter.

I know he didn't. He ain't even capable. Man wouldn't hurt a fishfly.

Joe Painter starts kind of scratching his arms and fidgeting. I can see the big black smear in the front of his pants now. He's shivering all ballistic and fevery, too.

You okay, Joe Painter?

Yeah, sure. I'm okay.

You sick?

He's like, I don't think so.

You don't look so good.

Last coupla days is all. Think I ate something funny. Bad mush or somethin.

I go, Bad mush?

Never know what they really puttin in it. It'll pass, Joe Painter says, clutching his stomach now. I ain't worried. Not really.

I go, Ain't you with the Syndicate?

I quit.

Even though he ain't really there, I can hear Oakley Brownhouse again. He's like, *You can't just quit the Syndicate, B.*

Joe Painter kind of hugs his stomach real hard like there's some glass breaking in his guts. Then he goes, They don't know I quit, but I did. Couldn't stand it no more.

I sort of stand there staring at Joe Painter like he's turnt into a werewolf or something.

After a minute, I go, If they catch you . . .

Joe Painter's like, I know, I know. That's why I'm buildin this, he says, pointing to the bodyboxes.

They're all funny-looking and broken down. Some have been joined together with these little metal things that look like hinges. I go, What is it?

Joe Painter kind of touches it real soft. He's staring at it all bright and crazyfaced like it's his best friend.

He goes, It's a boat.

I'm like, A *boat*?

Joe Painter nods and says, I'ma cross the Red River with it.

You are?

Yep. You wanna come? Could use the help rowin.

I'm like, Go *with* you?

Joe Painter says, I could even make a extra oar. Make it right over there on the planin table.

I'm like, You sure you're all right to paddle, Joe Painter?

As all right as I'ma get.

Joe Painter kind of shivers a little and adjusts his winch and points at the bodybox boat.

I'm leavin tomorrow mornin. Like I said, I could use the rowin power.

I imagine the two of us in the bodybox boat. Just floating across the Red River without nothin. Me with a paddle, pushing hard against the water, clunking the voodoo fishes that try to jump in the bodybox boat. And Joe Painter with his big thick mansmells, his hotspots all dark and purple, that glass breaking in his stomach. Wondering if it's Blackfrost that's causing those black smears in the front of his pants. No food. No safe jam. Just our paddles and the sound of the Red River taking the rain. Just each other.

I sealed her and everything, Joe Painter says, lifting the bottom so you can see all this tar that was smeared.

It smells like something that's been rotting in the Pits.

I already took half of it down to the Red River and tested it myself. All I gotta do is join this part here, he says, pointing to a stray bodybox that looks like some kind of storage space for blankets and food and water and tins of safe jam.

I imagine Oakley Brownhouse stepping toward the body-box boat and kind of putting his hand on it. He holds it like that for a minute and then for some reason he gets *in* it.

In my mind I'm like, *What are you doin, Oakley Brownhouse?*

He looks up at me with this scrunchnosed expression on his face and goes, *Testin it out, G. I ain't goin on the Red River in no galldangin shoebox. Wind up like some fishfood.*

Then, even though he ain't even really there, Oakley Brownhouse does something completely honking crazy. He lies down in the bodybox boat and he crosses his arms over his chest and he starts pretending he's *croaked*.

Me and Joe Painter just kind of stare at each other. I look back at the bodybox boat to see what Oakley Brownhouse is up to, but when I look he ain't there no more.

Joe Painter goes, So whattaya say? Wanna go with me?

I don't know what I'm going to say, and just when I think I'll sit down and get sleepy, my mouth opens and I'm like, Sure. I'll go with you, Joe Painter.

That night I dream of a flying thunderhorse. Its wings is huge and black and it comes diving through the Creature Clouds. At first I think it's a hawk or a falcon cause with my dream mind I remember what falcons looked like from that picture book at the Holy Family Agency, but then you can see its nostrils snorting all hot and smoky like they're going to shoot fire. The thunderhorse gets bigger and bigger and you can see its eyes and how they're mean and red and how they're so red it's like there's two hearts beating raw and bloody in its head. And that woman from the big black car with the clown makeup is riding it and she's smiling this huge snaggletoothed smile and in her arms she's petting a ditch dog. It's that ditch dog with the crooked leg that Oakley Brownhouse tried to kick to death. It's growling and showing how sharp and yellow its teeth is. The thunderhorse flying and its red eyes glaring bloody and the smell of it crashing down on me with its hooves and its fiery nostrils is all driving right into my little red curly head.

We gotta go, Thirty-three! someone says, shaking my shoulder. Gottagogottagogottago!

I forget where I am. I'm like, Huh?

Upnattem, girlie, upnattem.

Upnwho?

Before they start patrollin the Shelf.

The words is too big. I'm like, There ain't no *trolls* on the Shelf.

There's the Syndicate. There's the ditch dogs. We got twinny minutes to get the boat on the water.

The *boat*?

The bodybox boat. Where's your head, Thirty-three?

I'm like, Oh, my head.

Then the dream comes back to me. The flying thunder-horse. The woman from the big black car. The little ditch dog with the crooked leg. Those raw bloody eyes. The nostrils shooting fire. The hooves crashing into my head.

Come on, girlie, rise and shinola.

I'm like, Shinola?

Come on, Thirty-three.

It's coming back to me. The rain. The Creature Clouds. The bodybox boat. Joe Painter and his mansmells. Joe Painter and all his hotspots burning purple on his neck. The black smears on the front of his pants. His sour breath.

Joe Painter pulls me up by my arms and goes, I found three extra tins of safe jam and I got that flap canopied so we'll travel dry as a bone. And them four jugs in the kitchencove is all brimmin with washed water. Stopped up with corks and everything. Old Tick Burrowman sure kept things up to snuff.

In my mind I'm like, *Tick Burrowman*. In my mind I'm like, *Poor old Tick Burrowman*.

Joe Painter goes, Eighteen minutes. Eighteen and countin!

He's all electric-looking and nervous. His hands is kind of clawing at his hotspots and every few seconds he starts hugging his stomach like glass is busting in his guts over and over again.

I get up out of my halfbed and smear myself with some safe jam from one of the new tins and walk out into the middle of the life hole where the bodybox boat's stacked. It looks like something you'd find under some old croaked bridge.

Seventeen and countin! Joe Painter says and sticks two paddles on the top of the bodybox boat. Seventeen, seventeen!

I listen for Oakley Brownhouse in my head, but he ain't there no more. It's like his voice got real small and skinny and slipped through a crack in the wall.

It feels like all the parts of my body is moving on their own. My hands and my arms and my fingers and my legs and my toes, even. They're all just helping Joe Painter pack the bodybox boat. We roll a few sheets of plastic and stuff them into the little spaces that's left. I make sure there's enough candles and cheese and roll the cheese in some old cloth.

Fourteen minutes, Thirty-three! Fourteen and countin . . .

THE RED RIVER

Your body will do more than you think it can.

Me and Joe Painter carry the bodybox boat through the Bone Trees. The wind is crying and the trees is creaking, and even though we're smeared with the safe jam and covered with scraps of plastic the rain *still* burns through.

The ditch dogs ain't been brought up out of the Pits yet and the only person we see is this man all the way down on the other end of the Shelf. He's carrying this big gas torch and it's making a big yellow halo over his head.

You can't really tell if it's still the middle of the night or early morning. I guess you can never tell that kind of thing at the Shelf cause of the Creature Clouds, but for some reason it's like we're moving in a lost hunk of time, like one of those parts of the doubleday when everybody's sleeping, even the *ditch dogs*.

Joe Painter keeps his little winch on his shoulder. He says he's keeping it just in case we get into trouble, and I know he means just in case I can't carry my load, but I don't drop my end once.

I know I'm a Undertwelve and I'm a girl and all that, but I carry the bodybox boat just as good as Joe Painter with all his spicy mansmells. I know he's sick and he don't have all of his manstrength, but he's at least twice my size and he's got all that practice dragging trees and being a Syndicate soldier.

Strength don't always come from muscles and size. Sometimes it comes from that stuff that hides in your spit. And sometimes it comes from the places in your head where your mind makes thoughts.

Me and Shale Bluehouse used to practice lifting stuff with the muscles in our brains. We tried paperclips and shoelaces mostly. We never really got nothing to lift off the floor, but once Shale Bluehouse said I made a fleafly jump off this unbreakable comb that we found.

Joe Painter keeps grunting and huffing and going, Good, Thirty-three, attagirl, and stuff like that.

I'm grunting, too. I'm grunting so much I think my toilet muscles is going to bust, but they don't. Some of the noises that come out of me ain't no noises you'd think a *girl* would make. The sounds that's coming out of my mouth is more like sounds from a *thunderhorse* or a *ditch dog*.

It feels like the bones in my arms is going to get pulled right through my skin.

Joe Painter carries his end backwards through the Bone Trees. He's breathing hard through his teeth and his arms is shaking and you can see his little hotspots kind of swelling on his neck.

I'm like, You all right, Joe Painter? You all right? but he just keeps going, Attagirl, Thirty-three, *attagirl*. I almost slip a gazillion times.

When we get about halfway through the Bone Trees we set the bodybox boat down and Joe Painter runs behind a tree and makes some dooks. You can hear him eating his screams and moaning. I ain't going to describe the sounds cause it ain't even right.

While I wait, I cup my hands over my eyes and look up at the Bone Trees. The Creature Clouds is all thick and blackbellied and the tops of the branches is like little skinny fingerbones reaching for the sky. And it ain't like they're reaching for stars or the Moon or something in space. It's more like they're reaching for *food* or *money*. It's like they're reaching out cause they're *hungry*.

Then this other completely ballistic thing starts happening. If you stare at them too long it seems like they're *moving around* or *running* or something. You walk and walk and walk but no matter how far you get you can't never get through the Bone Trees cause they keep moving too. The only thing that stops the trees from running is Elton the Elephant. He's a gazillion feet in the air and you can't tell how many trees away he is, but you can see him. He's still at the top of the tallest branches and he's just sitting there like he climbed the tree by himself and just got tired and needed to rest. You can see the rain kind of dancing off the top of his big flat elephant head.

All the parts of him is still attached—his legs and his nose and his tail. Even his big goofy *ears* is still there. And when you think about it, it almost seems like he's looking for something.

Maybe it's cause of how his head's leaning forward, how his trunk's kind of sniffing the air. For a minute I think that maybe he really *is* up there looking for Gil. Somehow looking at him makes you feel better. I ain't sure why. I guess it makes you feel better cause it makes you think of Honeycut.

The sad thing is that Elton the Elephant's changing *colors*. He's kind of turning rusty like one of those old pennycoppers you find sometimes. There's still lots of silver parts, like his tail and one of his ears that's kind of bent, and the end of his trunk's silver too, but the rest of him is changing. It's like he's getting *sadder* or something. And that don't make no sense cause of how Tick Burrowman told me about how aluminum ain't supposed to rust. The rain must be pretty poisonous to make Elton the Elephant change *colors*.

After Joe Painter finishes dooking he comes walking out from behind the trees a little slow and wobbly. There's huge black circles under his eyes and his face is this funny yellow color. All of the sudden it's like *everything*'s changing colors.

I go, You sure you can do this, Joe Painter?

He's like, Ain't nothin in this world stoppin me now and that's all there is to it.

He takes a minute to cough and shiver and hug his stomach, and then he's like, Upnattem, Thirty-three, upnattem, and we count to three and lift the bodybox boat and it feels like we're lifting a *house* or a bunch of dead *thunderhorses*.

I walk straight and strong and don't even *think* about slipping.

Even though he ain't really there, I can hear Oakley Brownhouse again. He's going, *Don't slip, G. Don't slip!*

Somehow picturing Elton the Elephant makes carrying the bodybox boat easier. It's like Honeycut's right there in case I fall.

The Red River is warm. It don't feel warm from a fire or warm from the Creature Clouds and it don't feel warm from some other warmer river making friends with it. It feels like it's warm cause a bunch of blood got dumped in it or something.

Me and Joe Painter is standing in water up to our waists. We're trying to level the bodybox boat and the smell off the river's like a big compost bin of guts and dooks and rotten toes. You can see the dead fishes floating and how their eyes is all open and spooky. It looks like the muscles in their lids got burnt off, or like God froze them that way cause they was watching something they wasn't supposed to watch. They're floating all dead and stiff like they're made out of wood, like Tick Burrowman made some wooden fishes on his planing table and sneaked down to the Red River one night and throwed them in.

You can see some voodoo fishes voodooing, too, but every time they swim close I just slap them away with my paddle.

After we get the bodybox boat leveled it starts buckling and sagging. For a second it looks like it's going to sink straight to the bottom, but it don't.

Joe Painter keeps calling the front of the bodybox boat the *prow* and he keeps trying to point it toward the other side of the river. Then he steadies the sides with his big hands and gets it to lay pretty flat. After it settles it actually looks like a real *boat* that got made by real *boatmakers*.

Joe Painter needs help lifting himself over the edge cause he don't got no strength left. He tries to pull himself up, but I got to get underneath him and push his butt cheeks real hard. It feels like I'm pushing *three* men and *six* butt cheeks.

I almost can't get *myself* in the bodybox boat cause pushing Joe Painter takes so much out of me, but I jump and pull and twist and turn and wiggle and shake and fight them big magnets in the middle of the earth with all the muscles in my bones and finally flop in.

It takes a minute to get seated right and we almost flip like four times, but once we're steady, Joe Painter screws the posts into the corners and drapes the plastic flap over the top.

The rain drums on the flap and it drums on the sides of the bodybox boat and it drums on the Red River like little drums drumming down from Heaven. If you look real close you can see the Creature Clouds reflected on the skin of the water. They look like a bunch of smoky, scrunchtwisted mattresses or something, like the twists of smoke is forever trapped in the top of the water. And there's all these patches of dead fishflies that make the river look like it's got a *scab*.

We stick the tips of our paddles into the mud and push out. With every push Joe Painter kind of huffs and grunts and by the screams he's eating you can hear how that glass is still busting in his guts.

I'm like, You okay, Joe Painter? You okay?

He's like, I'm good, I'm good. Ain't felt better in the longest.

The truth is he ain't no better than the oldest, weakliest Elder or the smallest, scaredest Undertwelve. All them muscles and mansmells don't mean *nothing*. I guess that's what happens when you get real sick like that. I'm pretty sure he's got Blackfrost and I know I got to be careful. When me and Shale was still at the Holy Family Agency this one Bluehouse nun called Sister Lee Mary would tell us about Blackfrost and how you couldn't get it through the air but how you could get it from *blood* and *spit* and *dooks* and *boogers* and stuff.

Sister Lee Mary called the germs that make you sick the *microbes*, but Shale Bluehouse called them micro*bugs*. He would call them microbugs and sneak up behind you and run his fingers all on your neck like they was microbugs running.

After a while I started calling the Blackfrost germs microbugs, too, just cause it was funner. Sometimes we would pretend we was croaking from Blackfrost and try and put invisible boogers on each other and scream murderscreams and fake croak like we was getting squeezed to death by a bunch of frankenstein vampires and stuff. That was about the funnest thing me and Shale Bluehouse ever did. It was even funner than when we tried to light his farts on fire with these old Christmas tree lights we finded in the junk room. Shale Bluehouse was always better than me at screaming and croaking.

The Red River is thick and warm and smells like metal. We're lucky there ain't no Syndicate soldiers patrolling the banks. We paddle out a ways.

Bones and fingers, I keep telling myself. *Bones and fingers* . . .

As you get further out you can't even see nothing in the water. And all you can hear besides the rain drumming and the wind whipping is our breath breathing and our grunts grunting and our paddleslaps on the water.

The bodybox boat buckles and clacks over the brown waves and sometimes it sounds like some bones breaking. It's hard getting used to how the bodyboxes is hinged together. Sometimes they feel like they're going to split apart and just start floating in a gazillion directions.

I sit at the front where there ain't too big of a buckle. Joe Painter folds his greatcoat over the seam so I can sit good. We packed safe jam and cheese and matches and the last of the candles and enough washed water and Oldmonday mush to last a halfweek.

Joe Painter sits in the back end so he can steer. He's got to lean to one side when he paddles and he keeps clawing at his hotspots but we still keep the bodybox boat moving forward.

Joe Painter leans and gasps and sort of stares out across the water like he's seeing something.

I watch him watching the water. That yellow in his skin's turning darker and darker. It looks kind of brown now. His shivers is getting faster and more electric-looking, too.

When you look across the river you can't see nothing but water. Water and more water. Like the brownish-gray skin of some huge sleeping dinosaur. So much water it's like it just crawls up the sky and turns into the Creature Clouds.

Joe Painter goes, This godforsaken river just keeps goin and goin. Then he coughs a long cough and spits this big honking lungpuddle in the Red River. He claws at his hotspots a little and goes, In the Syndicate when they was trainin us they was always tellin you not to stare at the river. Hollerin at you like it's against the law or somethin. They say if you stare at it too much it'll make your mind weak.

I'm like, How come, Joe Painter?

Cause it tempts you.

Tempts you with what?

Toptown. Sunshine. Girls. Anything there is, I guess.

I'm like, *Mermaids?*

He goes, Maybe, Thirty-three. Mermaids would be kinda nice.

I'm like, Well, does it?

Does it what?

Tempt you.

Joe Painter goes, I don't know, and just keeps paddling and staring out at the water like he's staring at the biggest thing he's ever knowed.

Then I go, What if I was a mermaid?

You ain't no mermaid.

How do *you* know?

Cause you're too little.

No I ain't!

You're gonna be a pretty one when you get bigger.

You don't think I'm pretty *now*?

Yeah, you're pretty as hell, but you ain't no woman yet. You hit fifteen or sixteen and you're gonna have to start carrying a stick to beat the men off you.

I paddle a little and go, Girls can be mermaids, too, Joe Painter.

No they can't. Besides you smell too good. Mermaids smell terrible.

What do they smell like?

Fish.

We're quiet for a while. I paddle and stare out kind of blank and empty. For some reason I feel real old in the bodybox boat and I don't even know what old feels like. It's like my bones have been around a lot longer than my heart and my brain. I know that don't make no sense, but that's the only way I can explain it. I don't feel like no Undertwelve, that's for sure.

Joe Painter starts coughing more and he's got to stop paddling cause his lungpuddles is getting too thick. He coughs and grunts and spits into the water.

I start thinking about Oakley Brownhouse again. I try picturing his little bony knees. What's crazy is that when I try to see *other* parts of him, like his face and his eyes and his crazy hair—when I try to see *that* stuff—all I can see is this big black spooky *hole* in my brain. For some reason the only thing the muscles in my mind is letting me see is his knees.

Joe Painter goes, You're kinda like me, ain't you, Thirty-three.

I say, Like you how?

His purple spots is all blistery and swollen. I think a couple of them is about to bust all over the bodybox boat.

Joe Painter's like, You don't got nobody.

I go, Guess I don't.

Yeah, me neither.

I paddle a little but I got to stop cause my hands start to hurt. They're all crampy and stiff and the rain spraying under the flap is making them itch.

I'm like, Now all I got is you, Joe Painter.

He just says, Yep.

Then for some reason I go, You gonna disappear on me, too?

I feel all hot and small when I say that. Like I want to just lean over and fall right in the Red River.

Joe Painter's like, I ain't goin nowhere.

You promise?

Only place I wanna go is as far away from the Syndicate as I can get.

You'll have to go like a gazillion miles to get there.

We get across this durn river and we'll be all right, I guaran-dumtee it.

He coughs some more and spits and then we're quiet again.

It's hard to stay quiet cause all you keep hearing is the drumming of the rain and the clacking of the bodyboxes and all that does is remind you how lost and ballistic-feeling everything is.

I'm like, Hey, Joe Painter, you think they got medicine in Toptown?

Medicine?

Yeah, like some special medicine. You know, for your lung-puddles and stuff?

He's like, I spose.

I watch the reflection of the Creature Clouds on the top of the water. They look like a bunch of big honking ghosts wiggling. I go, You think they got *Blackfrost* medicine?

Joe Painter stares at me funny and says, You think I got Blackfrost?

I ain't sayin that. I mean, just in case one of us was to catch it. Like from the *water* or something.

Well, I gather that they got just about everything there is to get over there in Toptown. They got the Sun and that's enough for me.

He coughs and spits and grabs at his guts. When he cries out he sounds like he's losing big chunks of his life. He kind of cries for a minute and then he seems okay and stares out at the water again. He looks real sad and lonesome staring out at the water like that.

I go, You can lay down for a minute if you need to, Joe Painter. I can paddle by myself for a while.

He just shakes his head and keeps staring out. Then he cries a little more and goes, Thirty-three, if I don't make it to Toptown I want you to do me a favor, Okay?

I'm like, Sure, Joe Painter. Sure.

. . . My hands is cold . . .

I take his hands and hold them.

. . . They feel like ice . . .

I rub my hands over his. I ain't never felt hands like that before. They feel all thick and cold and rubbery.

He stares into my eyes and goes, If I don't make it, Thirty-three, I want you to drop me in the river . . . You hear me?

I hear you.

I don't want them Syndicate bastards to ever get me, understand?

I nod.

You just push me over the edge and keep on paddling.

For some reason I'm crying now. My face is hot and my throat feels like it's closing.

After a minute we start paddling again. We go silent for a long time. Just me and Joe Painter and the Creature Clouds and the rain coming down kind of leany and soft and the slow slooshing noises of the bodybox cutting through the Red River.

We talk a little bit here and there but it's like our words is being eaten by all those other sounds.

I can't even tell you what the last thing Joe Painter said to me was. It might have been something about the Sun or Toptown or it might have been about the taste of chicken and collyflowers. Whatever it was, it must have not been too important cause I can't even remember it.

The only thing I can remember is him saying how his hands was cold and how he couldn't feel his legs too good. I think it might have been them microbugs eating away at him, but I didn't say that. He poked himself in the backs of his legs a few times and said they was all cold and sandy-feeling. But then he just tried to lean in a different direction like if he did that the feeling would come back into them or something.

All I remember is what Joe Painter said about his legs and how I felt more tired than I ever been in my life and how the sound of the Red River making its little brown waves just made me more sleepy. We both put our paddles up and leant back.

It felt like we was out on the Red River for years. The minutes was like hours and the hours was like halfweeks. It felt like we was growing real old on that bodybox boat. Like we was turning all long and thin and gray.

When I waked up I was so hungry it felt like the wind was blowing in my stomach. My hands ached from rowing and I had to pee real bad. I ain't sure how long I slept but it must have been a while cause when I looked out over the Red River I could see a sliver of land where the Red River met the sky. It looked like there was some huge sleeping animal laying in the water.

I dropped my pants and kind of squatted over the edge of the bodybox boat to pee, and while I was peeing I got so excited at seeing the land I was like, *The Forsaken Lawn, Joe Painter! The Forsaken Lawn!*

I finished peeing and pulled my pants up and I said it again, and I said it even louder this time, *It's the Forsaken Lawn, Joe Painter!* but Joe Painter just kept sleeping.

I almost felt bad trying to wake him up cause he looked real peaceful sleeping there at the back of the bodybox boat. It was like he was having this dream about being somewhere he always wanted to go; like he was on one of those old slope-backed regular horses you used to hear about before the Creature Clouds came, and he was maybe carrying a bag that held all the small important things in his life, like some half-knots and some tins of safe jam and maybe a picture of a friend or something. And he was holding his bag over his shoulder and riding off into the sunset and whistling a song about how much he liked eating chicken and collyflowers. I ain't sure why

I thought that *that* was the dream he was having; that's just what popped into my head.

I cupped my hands over my mouth to make the sound bigger and shouted, *Joe Painter! Joe Painter, check it out! The Forsaken Lawn! The Forsaken Lawn!* but he still didn't wake up so I got down on my hands and knees and crawled over to him real easy and slow.

I was careful not to move too much where the seams was buckling and I was careful not to knock none of the posts that was holding the plastic flap cause the rain was starting to come harder now and the last thing we needed was for the canopy to get torned or ruined.

When I got close I had to cover my mouth cause of the smell. I knowed he was sick and I knowed he might have Blackfrost and I figured he probably ain't had no self-clean in a long time, but that smell was the worst smell I ever knowed. The only way I can describe it is by saying that it was so bad it felt like a old spooky invisible *hand* was moving through me. Like it was moving right through my guts and my toilet muscles. I put my hand over my mouth and ate the burps and puke and spit that was trying to fly up my throat and with my other hand I took Joe Painter's big honking paddle and kind of nudged him real soft. But he didn't move and he still had that dreamy look on his face so I nudged him again—this time harder. But he still didn't move, so I took the paddle and I kind of clunked him over the *head*. I clunked him hard and I clunked him fast so it made a old hollow wooden sound and that's when I knowed. It was like I was clunking something lost and broken. Like a thing that some kid finds in a basement and then starts clunking it with a stick or some metal just cause he can.

I knowed cause that look never changed on his face. I knowed cause them black smears in the front of his pants was so big they looked like places you see when you look at *maps* and old *globes*. Like those places got burnt or destroyed by big *blasterbombs* or something.

And I knowed cause that big spooky invisible hand was still moving through me all slow and achy and cold-feeling.

Joe Painter was croaked and it seemed like that was the only thing in the world I ever really knowed.

Joe Painter was croaked and the sliver of land kept getting bigger and bigger. All I could do was just sit there and stare at his body. It was funny cause it was like I was staring at a thing, like a old rusty bike or a stack of lost *books* or something, not no man.

You could almost feel how the bodybox boat was getting pulled toward the Forsaken Lawn, like God was blowing us there with his big windy Holybreath or something, like he was actually *helping* us for a change.

But just as those Godthoughts started making me feel a little better I seen something and I got this feeling like bad things was happening all over again. As the bodybox boat got pulled closer to that landsliver you could start to see twists of things kind of reaching off the top like a bunch of crazy *monkeyhairs* or some huge honking *snakes* that got froze in the sky. And when I looked even closer and kind of thought about it I realized it was the *Bone Trees* I was seeing.

For some reason I started talking to Joe Painter real fast. I knowed he was croaked and all but I was like, Joe Painter, Joe Painter, we're goin the wrong *way*! Grab your paddle, Joe Painter! Grab your *paddle*! and then I grabbed my paddle and started hacking in the water all ballistic and crazy like I was trying to kill the *river* or something.

That whole time we was sleeping we was just getting pushed back toward the Shelf and away from the Forsaken Lawn. Just when you think God is about to change, just when you think he might give you some good luck, he always pulls a fast one on you.

I just hacked and hacked at the water with my paddle and it was like I was hacking at the whole stupid honking *lost world*. I know I was talking to Joe Painter, too. I was saying more stuff like *Paddle, Joe Painter!* and *God tricked us! He* tricked *us, he* tricked *us, he* tricked *us!* and other crazy things. I think I even started shouting Honeycut's Chocolate Funfun Song real fast and ballistic. I was like, *Chocolate funfun gimme lots of fun Chocolate funfun gimme lots of fun* over and over and over again.

After I lost my paddle in the Red River, I realized that it was almost impossible to make the bodybox boat move with all the weight in it. That's when I decided to do what Joe Painter had asked me to do and dump him over the side. He weighed a gazillion tons and I know that his deadness didn't help none, but I used all the muscles in my hands and all the muscles in my legs and all the muscles in the smallest parts of every bone in my body and I leant and pushed and twisted his arms and legs and head and Syndicate boots over the side. There was all these big honking tears sliding down my face and they was hot tears like they was getting cooked by the fire behind my eyes, but I didn't care no more. I didn't care about nothing and I just watched Joe Painter's nasty stinky twisted dooksmeared body plop down and disappear.

I was as lonesome as I've ever felt but I couldn't just sit there in the bodybox boat and float so I grabbed his paddle and started hacking at the Red River. I was digging into the water as far and as hard as Joe Painter's paddle would let me, but it seemed like the harder I hacked the closer I got to the Bone Trees. The muddy muscles in the Red River was too strong for me and the bodybox boat. They was too strong for a Undertwelve girl even if she *was* using every muscle in her body and even if she *didn't* care about nothing no more.

Those tears was making me mad and I started yelling. I was like, *Stop crying, sissychicken! Stop crying, sissychicken!* But no matter how loud I yelled at my tears they just kept streaming down like the Creature Clouds got into my brain and started making poison burn out of my eyes.

After a while I just throwed the other paddle in the water and watched the Red River swallow it.

I could start to see the voodoo fishes voodooing again. I hated those voodoo fishes. At that moment I hated them more than anything.

The Bone Trees was getting bigger like they was made out of plastic shapes that some big huge monster was filling with air.

Right then I knowed I wouldn't never leave the Shelf whether I was staying in someone's life hole or hiding in a compost bin or whether I got clinched and sent to the Pits with all the Digit Kids. Something hot and small and sharp— something that was so small it could hide in the pipes where your blood flows—something like that knowed that I wouldn't never see Toptown.

MURDERER

I pulled the boat to shallow water with Tick Burrowman's mattock stick. I stopped for a second and just stared at it. It made me sad and a little sleepy cause it was like the mattock stick was one of Tick Burrowman's legs or something. I couldn't help thinking about how he got clinched and took away in the Flying Fox and how he would use the mattock stick to scrape the fishflies off the trees and how he would sometimes make his eyes pop and how he would dance with the mattock stick all slow and swervy like it was a woman.

The bodyboxes was clacking and buckling like crazy. I was lucky that there wasn't no Syndicate soldiers patrolling the banks of the Red River.

The rain was stinging my cheeks and I could feel little blisters blistering on my neck and ears. I took a jug of washed water, some cheese, and two tins of safe jam and rolled it all in the plastic flap. I twisted it tight and then poked the end of Tick Burrowman's mattock stick through the twistknot so I could carry it over my shoulder. I had to walk through the shallow water and for a minute I couldn't feel my feet. I felt so heavy and thick it was like I was walking in some big honking space boots.

When I finally made it to shore I just plopped down in the mud and catched my wind. There was dead fishflies every-where and they was all torched to blackness.

The Bone Trees was creaking and when I got to the first one I kind of fell down and *hugged* it. I ain't sure why. It wasn't like I missed the Bone Trees or nothing corny like that. It was more like hugging it stopped this feeling I was starting to get that a big black hole was going to appear in the Creature Clouds and suck me up into outer space. Somehow hugging that tree was like hugging somebody's *leg* or something—like a friend who will just stand there and let you hug his leg as long as you want.

So there I was, hugging that Bone Tree, when I heard this whipping noise. It sounded like a little flag flapping in the wind. I looked up and I seen this piece of paper that was sta-pled to the bark. It was a poster and there was a picture on it and a big number One underneath the picture. Above the pic-ture it said MURDERER in big black letters. I couldn't tell what the picture was at first cause of all the rain blowing in my face, but after I cupped my hands over my eyes I could see that it was a black and white photo of *Honeycut*. He was just stand-ing there all lost and scared-looking. It was kind of funny cause by the picture you couldn't tell how big and blobby he was. He looked like some regular Lost Man standing there. But the way they did it made his eyes look all hard and scary like he was some kind of *killer* or *evil frankenstein vampire* or something. Just looking at it made me feel all spooky inside. When I looked up I could see that there was Honeycut posters on a *gazillion* Bone Trees, and they *all* had Ones on them and they was *all* making them little flapping noises. It sounded like a gazillion Undertwelves was snapping their fingers real fast and angry.

Something inside made me wanted to tear down every poster from every Bone Tree but I didn't cause I knowed that that kind of ballistickness would get me clinched. So I tore down the poster from the Bone Tree I was hugging and I folded it and put it in my pants.

Walking through the Bone Trees with all of those Honeycut posters popping was one of the scariest things I ever done. I usually ain't scared by stuff like that, but the rain and the Creature Clouds and that clacking sound from the bodybox boat and Joe Painter plopping into the Red River made everything scarier. So I started kind of running, even though my body wasn't working too good and I was all heavy and cold from walking through the Red River. I runned as fast as I could and I tried to make all those sounds leave my head.

I finded a small compost bin at the other side of the Bone Trees. There was all these sticks and old newspapers in front of it and you couldn't see it too good if you wasn't looking, but I seen the door. There wasn't no buckle latch on it so I kicked it open.

I was feeling real sick and the first thing I did when I got inside was close the door and drop to my knees and puke. I know that ain't too smart cause I was going to have to sleep next to it, but I couldn't help it.

That's when I heard the voice.

It went, No dookin in here!

I was like, I ain't *dookin*, I'm *pukin*.

And the voice was like, No *pukin* nuther!

I said, Okay, okay. *Sorry!*

Then the voice said, Don't be so *sen*sitive, G.

I went, *G?!*

I puked again and then burped and I think I might have even farted cause I was laughing so hard.

I couldn't believe my ears.

THE SALT MAN

Oakley Brownhouse lost his Syndicate slacks.

He was in his underwears and his legs was folded into his chest all skinny and ballistic. There was a big mudblob covering his digits and when I asked him about it he said he'd been keeping mud on his digits so he wouldn't pick at them no more. He also said some Lost Man from another compost bin stealed his Syndicate slacks. He said the man had a fork and he was going to stick him in his neck if he didn't give them up. His underwears was all loose and dirty and you could see his dinkernuts if you looked real good but I only looked once and that was a accident.

He used two new candles to light the inside of the compost bin. They was taller than thumbs and burnt a pretty good light. He said he finded them in the Bone Trees when he was hiding from the ditch dogs. They was wrapped in plastic and lying on the ground like somebody dropped them. I told him he was lucky that they wasn't Undertwelve bait. Sometimes the Syndicate'll do that. They'll set a kite or a spongeball on the ground and clinch you when you go for it. After a while you learn how to ignore toys and stuff like that. Even though you want to grab that kite and run and run and run and make it fly as high as the Creature Clouds, you learn how to croak that thought.

Inside the compost bin there wasn't no dooks or garbage or nothing dead. It was strange being in a clean compost bin. It was more like something a *dog* or a *midget* would live in. Oakley Brownhouse said it was brand new and that as soon as he seen the Syndicate soldier unload it off the collection wagon and head back toward the Pits, he snucked out from behind the Bone Trees and rolled it on its side and dragged it into the shadows, where he covered it with sticks and old newspapers and big hunks of spoiled bark. The compost bin was so new that it didn't even have no buckle latch yet. He said he hided it so good that even the *ditch dogs* couldn't find it with all them brains in their noses.

I told Oakley Brownhouse about how I went back to Tick Burrowman's and how Joe Painter croaked from Blackfrost and how I left his body for the mermaids and how his body plopped into the water and sank to the bottom of the Red River.

Oakley Brownhouse was like, *Damn, G, damn*, and then I told him how the muscles in the Red River kept sucking the bodybox boat back toward the Shelf and how I lost my paddle and how I just gave up fighting the water after a while and let the waves pull me back with the dooks and the dead fishes.

I told Oakley Brownhouse how the bodyboxes was still

probably clacking and buckling somewhere all alone on the Red River like some ghosts was ghosting away in it.

He was like, You run into any blobfishes?

No.

Mudsharks?

Um. I don't think so, Oakley Brownhouse.

What about the Slowneck?

The *Slowneck*?

Hells yeah, G. Galldangin thing'll slide up underneath you and swallow you *whole*. They say it looks like a giant *jumpsnake*.

I was like, What the heck is a jumpsnake?

I don't know, but I bet it ain't no *regilar* snake.

That is so honking . . . *I don't know what*, Oakley Brownhouse.

They say that instead of a nose the Slowneck's got a *toe*.

A *toe*!

Yeah, G. A big greasy *grilla* toe.

A gorilla toe?

Yeah, that.

I was like, Instead of a *nose*?

That's what they say.

You don't even know what a gorilla *is*.

Oakley Brownhouse swallowed something in his throat and went, Yes I do.

What is it, then?

Huh?

You heard me.

He kind of snorted and cleared his throat and was like, *You* don't know.

Yes I do. I seen pictures of one in this book at the Holy Family Agency. They had *gorillas* and they had *elephants* and they even had these things with big long necks called *giraffes*. So there.

He didn't say nothing after that.

I went, A gorilla's like a *monkey*. A big crazy *monkey*.

Then Oakley Brownhouse went, Monkey *this*, and grabbed his butt cheeks with both hands.

I was like, You're so honking crazy I don't know *what*, Oakley Brownhouse.

He went, I'm serious about the Slowneck, G. You think I'm frontin?

You seen it?

No.

Well.

But I heard about it from this kid in the Pits. Kid called Bald Walt. Said the Slowneck swallowed both his parents when they was walkin down by the Red River. Said it came right up outta the water like a giant jumpsnake.

I was like, You got nothin but blobfishes on the brain.

My assbone.

Blobfishes, jumpsnakes, and your assbone. That's all you talk about.

I talk about other stuff.

No you don't.

Yes I do.

Like what?

I talk about all *types* of stuff, G.

Stuff stuff stuff. What stuff?

Like asternuts.

I was like, *Asternuts*?

Yeah, G. Them guys who chill on the Moon.

You mean *astronauts*.

Astronauts, asternuts, same differents.

You wanna be a astronaut, Oakley Brownhouse?

I don't know. I guess. I like them suits they wear. Them big silver things with the airconditioning.

The gravity suits.

Yeah, them. And that food they get to eat. In the little plastic bags and stuff.

Ick.

And you never know what you'll find on the Moon.

Looks all dead and lost to me.

Like maybe there's a bunch of kids up there.

Kids?

Yeah, G. Like a buncha lost kids hanging out in a Moonfield or something.

A *Moonfield*?

I'm just sayin, G. Like all them Undertwelves from the Pits.

Them ones who wind up in them bodyboxes.

What the heck is a *Moonfield*?

Like a field, G. You know. A *field*. On the *Moon*.

Okay.

And they're like playing this big game on the Moonfield and everyone's kind of running around and smacking each other on the head and drinkin chocolate milks.

I went, *Chocolate milks?*

Yeah, G. You ain't never had no chocolate milk before?

That stuff is so gross.

He went, I could drink chocolate milk *all doubleday*.

Makes me fart.

Makes me fart, too, G. But I wouldn't drink nothin else if I had me some.

Then we was quiet for a long time. You could start to smell how Oakley Brownhouse ain't had no self-clean in the longest. He smelled kind of like bad cheese. I didn't care, though. I didn't care cause I knowed I probably smelled too.

I was like, Hey. Oakley Brownhouse.

Huh.

Tell me somethin.

He was like, Okay.

About all them kids from the Pits . . .

Yeah?

The ones who wind up in the bodyboxes . . .

Uh-huh?

You think they go to the Moon after they . . .

I don't know, G. Maybe.

Then we was quiet again. You could hear the rain simmering on the trees and you could hear it simmering on the front of the compost bin and it felt like it was simmering inside you.

After a while I was like, Hey, again.

Oakley Brownhouse turnt to me but he didn't say nothing. He just stared at me. He stared at me and his eyes was huge and he was staring at me so hard it was like if he closed his eyes he would disappear.

I just looked at him. I looked at him so hard I thought I was going to start seeing his *bones* or something.

I said, You think we'll see each other up there in that Moonfield?

Oakley Brownhouse didn't answer and I didn't say nothing neither. He just kept staring at me with his big lost eyes and I kept staring at him. I thought I seen him nod his head but I couldn't tell you for sure.

He scratched the mudblob on his shoulder and started wiggling his knee. He watched me watching him and scrunched his nose and it was like me and Oakley Brownhouse wasn't apart for no time at all. His hair looked all crazy and pointy. It was like someone grabbed a fistful and just slashed at it with a *sword* or something. I reached over and fixed one of the new candles cause it was about to fall over. Then we didn't say nothing for a while. He kept looking at me all scrunchnosed and crazyfaced.

I was like, What's wrong with *you*?

He went, You *smell*.

I smell!

No kidding, G.

You should see your underwears! And what happened to your *hair*?

He was like, I chopped it.

Chopped it with what?

Piece of glass I found.

A *piece* of *glass*?

He went, Yup, and then he showed me this little piece of pointy glass and went, Ain't nobody gonna mess with Oakley Brownhouse again. They go for my shirt I'll stick em quicker than Sunday, I ain't lyin. Then he put the piece of glass back wherever he was hiding it and started shivering.

I went, How come you cut your hair?

He was like, Cause I was gettin bugs, that's how come.

Bugs?

Boogybugs.

Boogybugs?

All in my galldangin ears.

Ain't never hearda no boogybugs before.

Well, you just did.

I ain't never hearda half the stuff you talk about, Oakley Brownhouse.

Boogybugs is them little things that look like spidermites, G.

Wheredja get the glass?

Finded it in that compost bin down by where the rim of the Shelf turns black. Stayed there for a coupla hours till this old goathobblin frogface sucker kicked me out. Kicked me right in my assbone. Like I was a *football*, G. Ain't been able to sit right since, galldangitall.

You learned how to pick the buckle latches?

Most of em is already picked. Boltman ain't quick enough.

I kind of reached out and touched his zigzaggy hair. Looks like you fell asleep on top of a bunch of busted *pop*bottles, B.

He pushed my hand away and said, Looks like you came walkin out of a *boogerswamp*.

I was like, I *did*, and I can only eat boogers now or I'll croak. But they're delicious so I don't mind at all.

That's *nasty*, G.

Lighten up, Oakley Brownhouse.

You lighten up.

We didn't say nothing to each other for a minute and I could feel myself smiling. Inside I was like, *I missed you, Oakley Brownhouse. I missed my little jungle lover.*

But outside, I went, Happy to see me?

He was like, Sure, G.

You miss me?

It took him a minute, but he said it. He went, Yeah, I missed you . . . Same way you miss a piece of cheese or some gum.

I was like, A *piece* of *cheese*?

If you lose it, I mean.

Or some *gum*?

Gum is *good*, G.

Ha!

You know what I mean.

I just let it go and went, Well, I missed you, too, Oakley Brownhouse.

He was like, You smell like a fish.

I was like, You smell like some *horseballs*.

That made him laugh so I laughed a little, too, and then I ate my laughter and kind of just sat there shivering in the candlelight.

I looked at the new candles and went, You got enough matches?

He nodded and pulled two small boxes out of his underwear.

Where'd you get those?

Offa that guy over there, he said, and pointed to this heap of something over in the corner. When you looked closer you could see this beard kind of crawling out of the heap. I think it was a Lost Man.

Who's that?

Some old guy. Calls himself the Salt Man.

That's the Salt Man?

He didn't look like the Salt Man to me cause he wasn't wearing his dumbhat. He looked more like the *Compost* Man or something.

Oakley Brownhouse went, Don't wake him up cause he don't never stop talking. And he likes lookin in your mouth.

He does?

Yeah, G. Last time he was up he kept askin me if I would open my mouth so he could look in my hole.

Your *hole*?

Says he can see stuff in it.

What kinda stuff?

Like birds and flowers and a bunch of golden *chickens* and stuff.

Golden *chickens*?

That's what he said.

I was like, Did you *let* him?

. . . Yeah.

You did?

Well, sort of.

What happened?

He started crying and shit so I closed it.

Weird.

I tried to rub the shivers out of my body. I was starting to feel real sick again and my face was getting hot.

After a minute Oakley Brownhouse was like, Wish we had some of them beans and franks.

I nodded.

He went, Got any food?

I opened my plastic roll and gave him a hunk of cheese and

some washed water and he glurped down the water.

When he was through drinking he went, I saw Blobfish boy the other doubleday. They was haulin him off in a wagon. He was cryin like crazy. Sounded like he was about four years old. I miss that big bastard.

I pulled out that poster of Honeycut with the number One on it and showed it to Oakley Brownhouse.

You seen this?

He nodded and pointed to the number One and went, Yesterday they had Twos on em insteada Ones.

You know what it means?

Oakley Brownhouse shaked his head and went, Can't mean nothin too good.

Then the Salt Man stirred in the corner and kind of coughed and with this voice that sounded like it was coming from the bottom of a pile of rags he went, They're gonna *do* him.

I was like, What?

He moved a little in his heap of rags and said it again: They're gonna do him.

I went, *Who's* gonna do him?

Syndicate, missy. If they put you on a poster it means they're gonna *do* you. Plain and simple.

I was like, What's that mean?

The Salt Man kind of rolled on his side and went, What's *what* mean?

Do.

Do means do.

I was like, Oh. Then to Oakley Brownhouse I went, What's that mean? but he just looked at me and shrugged his shoulders.

Then the Salt Man was like, They usually do you down by the river. Them Syndicate bastards love their ceremonies. Turnin a do into a social thing and all. Then to Oakley Brownhouse he went, Hey, Little Jimmy, you find any more plastic?

Oakley Brownhouse was like, Nuh-uh. I ain't been outside yet.

You got any extra plastic, missy?

I nodded and kind of crawled over to him and tore some plastic off the flap. I handed it to him and he folded it up real tight and tucked it somewhere under all of his rags and papers. The heap stunk horrible. You could smell the sweet warm smell of his breath and his sweat and all of his dooks, too. I felt real bad for him when I smelled that.

He looked at me and went, What's your name, missy?

I was like, Whensday.

Whensday, huh?

Yes sir.

Could you do me a favor, Whensday?

What kinda favor?

Lemme look in your hole.

Oakley Brownhouse was like, See, G? I *told* you.

I was like, My *hole*?

Your mouth, love.

Um . . . I looked at Oakley Brownhouse, who was looking back at me with this big honking blank expression on his face.

Jes' for a second, missy. I ain't gonna hurt you.

Why you wanna look in my mouth?

Cause I can see things.

What kinda things?

Things you don't never forget. Colors. Waterfalls. Twirly-birds.

Twirlybirds?

Saw three golden chickens in Little Jimmy's mouth. Two mommahens and a roostercock. Golder than a fielda wheat on fire. You ever seena fielda wheat catch fire?

Nuh-uh.

Purest gold you'll ever see. Golder than gold.

I looked over at Oakley Brownhouse, who was kind of warming his hands over his new candles.

The Salt Man went, After Little Jimmy swallowed them golden chickens I saw a three-legged turkeybird jumpin on his tongue. Dancin a jighop right ona fronta his esophygossy.

. . . You did?

Hoppin on one leg and smilin like Sweet Tooth Freddie with a pocketfulla candycanes. Saw a coupla ducks, too.

To Oakley Brownhouse I was like, He seen *ducks* in your mouth?

He says he did.

The Salt Man went, Please, love. I don't want no more plastic from you and I ain't hustlin for no food. I jes' wanna look in your pretty little hole. I swear I ain't gonna hurtya.

I looked over at Oakley Brownhouse and he just shrugged all lost and slumpy-looking. The candlelight was sawing on his face and the shadows was making him look old and sad.

To the Salt Man I was like, What happened to your hat?

Huh?

Your dumbhat.

Oh, that old thing? I ate it.

You *ate* it?

Fella's gotta eat something. Found a little jar of peanut butter down by the Red River. Gussied her up and gobbled her down. Tasted pretty fair, too. Ain't been able to stand right since, but it took care of the whistlin in my ribs.

I bent down and the Salt Man lifted hisself up out of his ragheap. With his face in the candlelight now you could see how his beard was all knotted and full of little pieces of garbage and the kind of things you find in your pocket.

His eyes was all black and spooky like two holes poked in a pumpkin. He only had about seven teeth and most of them was all rotted. He looked more like a Lost *Ghost* than a Lost Man.

When you got close the smells was even worse. All warm and thick and nasty enough to make your throat close. But I just stood there and kind of leaned over him. He reached up real gentle and took my face in his hands and they was soft and warm and dry. I opened my mouth for him and he stared into it for a long time. I ain't sure how long it was, but it was so quiet and still that you could almost hear the rain *thinking*. And those rainthoughts wasn't thoughts with words and pictures; they was the kind of thoughts that give you a *feeling* and that feeling was all lost and sad and empty like when it's real cold out and you're tired from walking and you can't find nobody and you see a big metal chair that someone left in the middle of the street and you decide to sit in it and maybe it starts to rain a little and you see some kid run by with a busted kite or something. I know that don't make too much sense, but that's how them rainthoughts was.

The Salt Man's eyes was like these big huge lost zeros. Then he started to smile this big honking ballistic smile and you could see all the different colors that was living on his seven teeth and then he started laughing and his laughter was so big it was like four men was laughing and they was laughing right into my mouth and then the laughter turnt to crying and it was like four men was crying right into my mouth and his eyes went kind of silver and cloudy and all these tears started leaking down his old dirty face and I just stayed there with my mouth open and his big warm hands holding my face.

His crying lasted for a long time. I couldn't tell if his tears was tears of fear or tears of gladness and after a while his crying got real small and quiet like a animal that disappears down a hole.

You could still hear the rain and how it was thinking and you could still hear the wind and how the rainthoughts was kind of twisting through it and you could hear how Oakley Brownhouse was fidgeting in the other corner.

I went, So what did you see?

The Salt Man took his hands away and shaked his head and smiled.

I was like, What?

His mouth was still open and he just kept shaking his head.

You see ducks and chickens?

He shaked his head.

You seen a big turkeybird?

He just kept shaking his head.

You didn't see no animals?

I saw a animal all right. Biggest animal I ever seen in my life.

What was it?

Big old trunk. Floppy ears. Crooked tail. Sitting right on the back of your tongue. Sittin there like it had seven different kindsa thoughts.

You seen a *elephant*?

Big old copper elephant. Just sittin there. Sittin there in the middle of a snowstorm.

I got sick three times that night. I was sure I had Blackfrost and I was going to croak. It was funny cause every time I

throwed up I got this taste in my mouth like a *flower* was growing in my stomach. And it was like that flower was making me
real hungry so I would eat a hunk of cheese and drink some
washed water real quick, but then I'd just feel all seasick and
hot and thick and throw up a few minutes later. It felt like my
body was turning into something it wasn't supposed to *be*, like
I was changing into a dog or a bushchicken or something.

Me and Oakley Brownhouse was huddled in the corner
cause it was starting to get cold. His little naked legs was going
ballistic. I wished we still had the greatcoat and I wished we
had some beans and franks to eat so Oakley Brownhouse
would quit crying about being hungry.

Oakley Brownhouse was like, It's too *cold* to be starvin, galldangitall!

I went, I know, Oakley Brownhouse, I know, I know, and we
just kept shivering into each other like we was getting stuck
with frozen needles.

Once Tick Burrowman told me how the weather was going
to change. He said one night the temperature would drop and
the rain would turn to snow and everything would freeze and
the snow would make everything look like a wedding cake.

For some reason I kept thinking about that doubleday when
Second Staff Brown was over at Tick Burrowman's life hole
and how he was talking about picking the Futurists. I kept
looking at Oakley Brownhouse and how he was shivering next
to me and I started thinking about that for some reason. I fig-

ured I'd only be around for a few more days, cause of how Blackfrost was croaking me, but I wanted things to work out for my little lost Digit Kid.

I went, W-W-What are you gonna do n-n-n-next, Oakley Brownhouse?

N-N-Next?

Yeah, next. Like with your l-*l-life*.

He was like, I don't know. What am I sposed to d-d-do?

You gonna hide in sodabushes and c-c-compost bins till you hit t-t-twelve?

He was like, I guess I ain't got no ch-ch-choice. I ain't goin back down to the P-*P-Pits*. Wind up in a b-*b-body*box.

We was quiet for a minute and all you could hear was our teeth chattering.

Oakley Brownhouse looked at me and went, What is *you* gonna do?

I was like, I ain't gonna be around much l-l-longer.

You ain't?

I think I'm sick, Oakley *B-B-Brown*house.

He went, I know. You're pukin like you drunk paint.

I think I got B-B-Blackfrost.

He looked at me real hard and went, But you don't g-got no hotspots.

I was like, I know, but I can't keep no ch-*ch-cheese* down and I feel all l-l-lopsided.

You got B-B-Buckfrost we can't be around each other, G.

I was like, I know, Oakley Brownhouse. I know. T-T-Tomorrow I wanna go back to Honeycut's life hole.

F-F-For what?

I left somethin there. I want you to c-c-come with me. After that we can split up.

He was like, You sure, G-G?

I'm sure.

We was both shivering and the Salt Man was coughing and outside the rain had picked up again. It sounded like it was raining harder than ever and I pictured the Creature Clouds kind of boiling all dark and ugly in the sky.

I went, Can you do t-t-twenty pushups, Oakley Brownhouse?

He was like, Huh?

I went, P-P-*Pushups*. Twenty p-*p-pushups*.

Oakley Brownhouse scratched at his mudblob and went, T-*T-Twinny*?

Yeah, twenty.

Like all at once?

Straight through without stopping.

Oakley Brownhouse picked his mudblob some more and was like, Hells yeah, G. Twinny p-p-pushups ain't nothin. I can do fitty of them things if I got a m-m-mind for it.

Let's see.

Let's see?

Yeah, show me.

Show you why, G-G?

I was like, Just c-c-cause, okay? Just cause.

. . . All at once?

I nodded.

. . . I ain't gotta p-p-prove nothin.

Just show me how many you can do.

You just wanna see my m-m-muscles.

No I don't.

All my hugeness and s-s-*s-strumf*.

Please . . .

You know you *do*.

I swear I d-d-don't, Oakley Brownhouse. I swear.

Well, I ain't *d-d-doin* it.

How c-c-come? It'll warm you up.

You're just gonna get all excited and start foamin at the m-m-mouth.

I went, Fine, then *don't* do twenty honking p-p-pushups!

The Salt Man kind of grunted and burrowed deeper into his ragheap.

Then Oakley Brownhouse started rubbing his arms real fast and ballistic and quickened his breath and peeled his little greasy T-shirt off and kind of laid on his stomach.

I went, What are you d-*d-doin*?

He was like, Well, if you're gonna be all s-s-*sen*sitive . . . and then he started doing pushups. His little skinny arms wobbled and it looked like his bones was going to bust through his shoulders. His face started shaking, too. He counted out the way soldiers do.

I was surprised when he got to ten and even more surprised

when he reached fifteen, even though he couldn't say nothing past twelve. His arms was shaking all ballistic and electric-looking and after fifteen he could only do two more. After seventeen he tried but his face was the only thing that was moving. His eyes was bulging so hard I thought they was going to pop. He gave up and just laid there on the floor.

After a minute he went, Twinny.

I was like, That was seven*teen*.

He went, I did *twinny*, ain't it, Salt Man? but the Salt Man didn't say nothing back. He was loving his plastic and his papers and he was sleeping the long deep sleep of someone who sees chickens and twirlybirds in other people's mouths.

Oakley Brownhouse put his T-shirt back on and made his face all hard and pouty.

I went, Seventeen ain't b-b-bad, Oakley Brownhouse. It ain't bad, but it ain't good enough.

Good enough for what, G?

The Syndicate.

He was like, The *who*?

The Syndicate. You show them you can do twenty pushups and they take you in. Make you a Futurist.

So?

So it might be something to look f-f-forward to.

I don't care if I could do a *gazillion billion* pushups, G. I ain't *never* joinin up with them suckers.

There's a future in it. Nice hot m-m-meals. Good clothes. All them shiny b-b-buttons. A thunderhorse of your very own. Just somethin to think about.

Think about *this*, he said and grabbed at his little dinky crotch.

That night we huddled close and our blood cooked up pretty nice and eventually our shivering stopped. Oakley Brownhouse's legs even stopped going ballistic. It got colder and you could feel how the air was changing.

I eventually fell asleep and dreamed of snow. It was the kind of snow that's so big it looks like paper dolls twirling down.

I waked up one time and puked into my hands. I was surprised to find Oakley Brownhouse still asleep next to me. His eyes was moving all quick behind his lids, like they was spinning a dream through the back of his mind.

After I got sick I fell back asleep and dreamed of snow again. This time it was like cake mix falling and you could eat it. I opened my mouth wide and filled my stomach and in my dream it felt like I would never have to eat again. The Salt Man was there too and it felt like we knowed each other forever and we looked into each other's mouths and seen incredible things.

The snow was warm like feathers and it was falling on top of Honeycut's elephant and his trunk was all white like God painted it that way and me and the Salt Man was holding hands and doing cartwheels and dancing through the Bone Trees.

The second time I waked up, Oakley Brownhouse wasn't lying next to me. At first it made me feel sad and small cause I thought he runned away again, but then I heard him grunting and huffing and after my eyes adjusted to the light I could see that he had lit one of the new candles and he was doing pushups. His little naked legs was so white they looked like they would be cold if you touched them. He was doing pushups in the halo of the candlelight and he was doing them five at a time as if his life depended on it.

THE TODAY DOUBLEDAY

The Honeycut posters didn't have no numbers on them no more. They still had his picture with MURDERER on it, but it said TODAY where the number One used to be.

They're gonna do him, I kept hearing the Salt Man say in the back of my head.

Do means do.

The new posters was pasted over the old posters and when we was weaving through the Bone Trees the wind was making them snap and pop and it was like the Bone Trees themselves had become angry and was clicking their treeteeth or something.

Oakley Brownhouse can't read too good so he kept asking me what it said.

I went, It says Today.

They're gonna *do* him, G.

Sh-sh-sh-sh.

Honeycut's a galldangin *outlaw.*

We runned and weaved and slipped in the mud. My mouth filled with puke but I spit it out and kept pumping my arms. Our plastic was loud and wet and dumb-sounding and it smelled like fishflies and compost bins and the skin of the Red

River and the smell was making me seasick and after a minute everything felt all thick and lopsided like I was walking through water again.

It wasn't snowing even though I dreamed about it. I thought I'd see them big paperdoll snowflakes spinning down but it was still raining and the rain was sideways and it was so thick you could have *drawed* it and it was so cold it felt like little wet metal *feet* running on your skin.

It was too early for the ditch dogs and the only person we seen was a Lost Man losting away through the Bone Trees. He was walking with his arms spread wide like he was trying to catch invisible halfknots that was falling from the Creature Clouds and he was singing this song all loud and horrible like he was going to *croak* or *explode*. He wasn't singing no words, he was just sort of howling and crying the song from his guts and no matter how fast we runned you could still hear him and his voice was making me feel even more lopsided and seasick. I had to stop and lean up against one of the Bone Trees and puke.

Oakley Brownhouse was like, It's too early to be upchuckin, G.

I just nodded and puked.

We kept walking and eventually the Lost Man's songvoice got swallowed by the rain and the wind and the thunder in the Creature Clouds.

That's when we seen Honeycut's life hole.

It was all boarded up and plastered with Astan Loe posters

and it looked old and wrecked and burnt and the more you stared at it the more it felt like it was going to *disappear* or something.

Somehow it suddenly got so quiet that all you could hear was the wind pulling at the posters and the rain kind of whispering its cold metal whisper.

It felt like everyone had gone away or something, like the whole world got clinched and sent to the Flying Fox and me and Oakley Brownhouse was the only ones left.

Just standing there in the quiet you could tell that a gazillion Syndicate soldiers went ballistic with a gazillion hammers and a gazillion nails and a gazillion pieces of wood. And you could tell that they did it in about four minutes too cause of how the nails was all zigzaggy and half-driven. When they was hammering all them nails it probably sounded like *war* sounds. It looked like they was trying to *croak* Honeycut's life hole.

You could tell Astan Loe was there too and you could just imagine how he was probably circling all their hammering on his big honking thunderhorse. It seemed like them posters was more important than boarding up the life hole cause of how clean and straight and perfect-looking they was. Astan Loe's eyebrows was hanging all mean and spooky over his eyes like some old rusty black knives you'd find in a *volcano* or something.

Oakley Brownhouse started kicking a hole in the wood. He was going, *Beans and franks, beans and franks*, and he was saying it all low and fevery under his breath. I tried using the mattock stick but it broke in two so I just throwed it down.

When the bottom of Oakley Brownhouse's shoe fell off it didn't matter and he just kept kicking and when the hole was big enough to poke our fists through we each grabbed a side and pulled and our pulling drove splinters in our hands but it didn't matter cause even though it was quieter than ever and wasn't no one around you could *feel* them watching you. You could feel the Syndicate watching you and you could feel the windsmoke from the nostrils of their thunderhorses crawling soft and invisible over the bones in your neck and you could feel the teeth from the ditch dogs going fast and electric behind their muzzlestraps and you could feel how the ditch dog teeth would bite through the muzzlestraps like they wasn't nothing but paper or candywrappers and you could feel how they would sink into the backs of your legs like big long fish-forks.

Oakley Brownhouse kicked some more and I picked the splinters out of my palms and then I kicked while he picked the splinters out of his. The rain was coming so fast it seemed like it was *singing*.

When the hole got big enough we wiggled through on our stomachs.

Inside it was so dark you couldn't even see your hand in front of your face. Oakley Brownhouse lit his candle and the little halo from the candlelight flared up and we could see the walls and the shadows on the walls and it was like the life hole had all these secrets it was trying to tell us, like maybe what it knowed about the rain and the Creature Clouds and the way God puts things on the earth and just messes them up when he feels like it. I don't even know if that makes sense, but that's what I kept thinking about for some reason.

We walked from corner to corner, but there wasn't nothing left. Oakley Brownhouse kept begging for Second Staff Brown's foodlocker and kind of praying for beans and franks and I kept telling him that the Syndicate took it back, but he wouldn't listen.

After I felt the wall for a few minutes, I finally finded the hole where I hided my nest.

That flower felt like it was crawling up my throat now and I couldn't swallow hard enough to make it go back down. I puked again and it felt like something deep in my guts came out with the puke, like one of those little food tubes that lives next to your toilet muscles. I don't think anything actually came out, but it *felt* like it did.

When I turnt around, Oakley Brownhouse was standing behind me and his hand was on my shoulder and he was crying like a big honking sissychicken.

He was like, Don't *up*chuck, G. Don't *up*chuck.

His eyes was huge and scared and in the candlelight they looked doublehuge and doublescared.

I squeezed my nest hard cause I wanted it to be the last

thing I felt before I croaked.

His upper lip started quivering and going ballistic and he was like, You gonna make it, G?

I was like, I don't know, Oakley Brownhouse. I think I'm gonna croak.

He went, Don't *croak*, G. Please don't croak.

He was so funny-looking right there in the weak light of the candle. His underwears looked like they got bigger and his little white legs was wobbling so much I thought they was going to pop off and just start walking away on their own. And his teeth was chattering so loud it was like they was chattering in my *ribcage*.

I went, Oakley Brownhouse?

He was like, Huh.

Would you do me one favor?

What kinda favor?

Just say yes. One favor before I croak.

Sure, G. I guess.

I got kind of sad for a minute. But not too sad. I don't even know why.

I went, Say my name.

He was like, Your name?

Yeah, my *name*.

He was like, Oh no, not *that* again.

If you say it it makes me feel like I'm still here, okay?

Whatever.

Like when you climb a tree and you're just lookin at a bird or the sky and then someone says your name and you look down and they're holding a busted kite or some *flowers* or somethin.

Flowers?

It's like hearin your name reminds you of those flowers and you can remember their *colors* and stuff. It's like you and the colors is the *same*, okay?

Oakley Brownhouse picked his nose and went, But I *always* say your name, G.

I was like, You *do*?

Yeah, G. You just don't never hear.

When do you say it?

I don't know, G. I just say it. I don't open my mouth but I say it.

You say it inside?

He went, Sort of. I guess.

Like you're prayin it?

I don't pray, G. Prayin's stupid.

It ain't stupid.

You don't pray.

So. That still don't make it stupid.

Ain't nobody listenin.

How do you know?

Just cause.

You ever try it?

Hells no.

Then how do you know?

You just *know* that type of stuff, okay?

We didn't say nothing for a minute and the candle was starting to burn down. The halo was getting smaller and smaller, which made the shadows darker and colder-looking.

I went, Oakley?

He went, G.

Would you say my name out loud? So I can hear?

Why?

Cause it's my birthday, that's why. It's my birthday, okay?

It's your galldangin *birthday*, G?

Yeah. Last night.

Last night?

Yeah, I almost forgot.

What was funny was that I *did* almost forget. It was like everything that happened made the days all blend funny. But when I counted backwards in my mind from the hundredth doubleday of rain it worked out that way.

Oakley Brownhouse went, So how old is you?

Twelve.

You're *twelve*?

Yeah.

You know what that means?

I know what it means.

It means they can't clinch you no more, G!

They can't clinch me but I'm gonna croak anyway so it

don't even matter.

You're so *lucky*, G.

I went, Croakin ain't *lucky*!

I mean about hittin twelve!

You can't even say happy birthday?

Oh. Happy birthday . . . damn, you're lucky.

Will you just do it, Oakley Brownhouse?

He didn't say nothing for a minute and you could hear the rain and it was like the rain was raining inside you, like there was a little Creature Cloud behind the bones in your chest and it was raining on your guts.

Oakley Brownhouse went, If I say your name it don't mean nothin.

I know.

It don't mean *shit*, you hear me?

I hear you.

Okay.

. . . I'm waiting.

Now don't start upchuckin from the excitement, gall-dangitall.

He couldn't do it at first. It was really sad.

I kind of pushed him in the chest with one finger and went, You got a heart, Oakley Brownhouse? but he didn't answer. He just kept shivering and chattering his teeth and picking at his digits.

I said it again. I went, You got a heart or a piece of *cheese* in your chest?

He went, I ain't got no galldangin *cheese* in my chest, Cheesy G.

You got no guts.

Do *too*.

Do *not*.

Do too, Sucker!

So far all I hear you callin me is Cheesy G and Sucker.

Then he started folding and unfolding his arms and biting his lower lip and I thought he was going to burn himself with the candle cause of how fast he was moving. And then this little squeaky fartblast popped out of his underwears and *that's* when he finally said it—after he farted.

He went, . . . *Whensday*.

I couldn't believe it. I couldn't believe Oakley Brownhouse actually said my name.

He was shaking harder than ever and I thought *he* was going to croak cause it took so much out of him. I thought his ribs was going to pop right through his little greasy dooksmeared T-shirt and start rattling by themselves on the floor.

When he said it I think I fell for him all over again. I think I fell for him again cause those feathers was tickling the muscles in my heart. They was tickling even though I felt all lopsided and seasick.

But I still thought he was a sissychicken. I still thought Oakley Brownhouse was a sissychicken cause of how he had to wait for the candle to go out so he could say my name in the dark.

STONES

The noise rose up like a swarm of fishflies breathing on you. The voices was like flames and they was burning right through the Bone Trees. Flamevoices of men murmuring low and burning low and feeling hot and thick and thunderfilled like they was fire rained down from the Creature Clouds. The way men's voices change and become one voice. The way the fishflies fly all hot and close together like one huge honking fishfly. The way a hundred faces can turn to one.

Me and Oakley Brownhouse was going back to the hidden compost bin where the Salt Man lived, but we heard the whistling. It was the first time I ever heard it and it *did* sound like a church song and it was such a good whistle it sounded like it was coming from the *radio* when there was still radios with songs on them. You could hear the Boltman's keys jangling too, like a bunch of little glass baby bones or something.

We turnt and headed for the Red River.

That seasick flower was getting thicker inside and my skin was turning cold and froggy and I just knowed my body was getting ready for croaking. Part of me still felt like I was on the bodybox boat and I could smell the Red River rivering and I think the smell was making that flower grow and I had to stop and puke again and again and again and Oakley Brownhouse held the back of my shirt so I wouldn't fall over and after I puked I felt better and we kept walking.

The voices got louder and you could hear the ditch dogs growling behind their muzzlestraps.

We stopped at the edge of the Bone Trees and ducked into a sodabush.

On the banks of the Red River there was a gazillion Syndicate soldiers all lined up in columns and they had their blasterguns on their shoulders and they was standing still and talking low and they looked like they was waiting for something to come walking out of the water. The buttons on their greatcoats was all shined up like money and their boots was polished and just looking at them made you feel kind of scared and sleepy.

I thought the sodabush was the right place to give Oakley Brownhouse my nest. I figured he could just walk up to one of the Syndicate soldiers and hand him my birthpaper and tell him that he was me, that he was Whensday Bluehouse from the Holy Family Agency when there was still a Holy Family Agency to be from.

So I gave Oakley Brownhouse my nest and I pulled out my birthpaper and I unfolded it and smoothed it on my knees.

Oakley Brownhouse looked at my birthpaper and went, What is it, G?

I told him what it was and I told him how the Holy Family Agency didn't never check the box next to Girl and how they didn't never check the box next to Boy neither. They didn't check *nothing*. I guess they forgot or maybe they didn't bother to look at my little baby privacy. I think it's funny how a piece of flimsy paper can mean so much in your life. It's like all those little numbers and boxes and words that get typed is just as important as your *bones* and your *heart*.

Then I gave my birthpaper to Oakley Brownhouse. He looked all lost and confused.

He was like, What am *I* sposed to do with it?

Walk up to one of them Syndicate soldiers and show it to him. They might take you in. Just think. Hot meals. Good clothes. Safe jam. All the beans and franks you can eat.

He was real scared and swallowed something in his throat and went, I don't know, G. I don't know.

At least think about it, Oakley Brownhouse. Promise me you'll at least think about it.

His voice got real small and he went, I'll think about it, G. I'll think about it.

Then we was quiet and you could hear the rain pattering on all the Syndicate helmets.

Oakley Brownhouse started feeling his arms. It was like he was checking to see if they got bigger. Then he went, What about you?

I'm gonna croak, Oakley Brownhouse. Can't you see that?

You really think you got Buckfrost?

I nodded.

You sure?

I nodded again. It was funny cause right then I thought I could almost *feel* my pee turning black in my guts. I just knowed that them black pee smears was about to start smearing all over the place.

Oakley Brownhouse looked at my birthpaper and said, I don't even know what this shit *says*.

Don't worry about it. Just don't lose it.

Oakley Brownhouse nodded and folded it in fours and pushed it back into the nest.

Out of nowhere this big horn honked all crazy and ballistic. It was so loud it was like something you hear before a blaster-bomb. The Syndicate soldiers and ditch dogs went quiet. It was like God took all their voices away with a wave of his hand or something. You could hear the Red River kind of sleeping and you could hear the rain running on the water and you could hear a horse clopping and a kind of squeaking. The horseclops and the squeaks got louder and louder and then you could see Astan Loe on his big black thunderhorse and directly behind him was about twenty Digit Kids and they was pulling the collection wagon. They was all white and hunched over and a bunch of them had scabs all over their arms and they was so skinny it was like they was some other kind of animal, like they was part *fish* or part *alleycat,* or something. Their bald heads was like little moons and they was all weak and tired-looking.

Some of them couldn't walk too good and even the ones

who wasn't limping had something else wrong with them like they had hotspots or one of their arms was just hanging funny or they was walking sideways. They was all dressed in black garbage bags and that just made their skin and their moonheads look whiter and sadder than they really was.

You couldn't tell who was girls and who wasn't girls and it was like their eyes was *bulletholes* or something. Some of them was wearing shoes and the ones who wasn't wearing shoes was wearing milk cartons on their feet and the ones who wasn't wearing milk cartons wasn't wearing nothing. They was chained together, ankle to ankle, and with every step you could hear the chains clanking.

When the collection wagon came into view it creaked and moaned and sounded like it had been pulled a gazillion miles. Honeycut was standing in the center. He had this big black bag over his head and he wasn't wearing nothing else except this piece of plastic that they tied around his waist to hide his privacy. I knowed it was Honeycut cause his stomach was huge and soft and dirty and underneath the black bag you could hear his voice and how he was kind of howling something. It was one word but you couldn't hear what it was cause the black bag was kind of eating the word. He was howling that word over and over again and it sounded more like the noise a sick *bear* would make in the back of a cave than something being howled by a man.

Behind Honeycut was this huge honking pile of stones and

they looked like Shelf rocks that got split and then split again and the rain had slicked them up so they almost looked soft.

When the collection wagon finally stopped Astan Loe rode his thunderhorse around the Digit Kids and with his black eyes he watched them all hard and angry the way you watch something that you want to throw off a *cliff*. The horseclops kind of echoed in the silence.

Behind us you could see a bunch of Lost Men kind of hiding in sodabushes and clinging to the trunks of the Bone Trees.

Honeycut was still howling out whatever it was he was howling and after Astan Loe finished riding his circle around everything he pointed to two Syndicate soldiers who was in the front line and then he pointed to Honeycut.

The two Syndicate soldiers saluted Astan Loe and he saluted them back and then they left their blasterguns on the banks and jogged over to the collection wagon. They each grabbed one of the chains that was holding Honeycut. Then Astan Loe rode his thunderhorse over to the collection wagon and he pulled this lever near the back and when he pulled it it made this big loud honking cracking noise and the back end of the collection wagon collapsed and all the stones tumbled onto the banks of the Red River.

Then Astan Loe rode back over to his place at the front of the ranks of the Syndicate and he pointed to two other Syndicate soldiers from the front line and they saluted him and he saluted them back and one of the Syndicate soldiers walked over to the Digit Kids and made them form a circle around the collection wagon while the other Syndicate soldier gathered rocks and started passing them out to the Digit Kids. He passed one rock at a time and each Digit Kid passed the rock down the circle till all the rocks was passed and each Digit Kid had a pile.

When they was finished dealing the rocks the two new Syndicate soldiers joined the other two Syndicate soldiers and grabbed the final two chains. There was four Syndicate soldiers holding the tetherchains now.

Honeycut was still howling in the wagon and, just for a minute, besides the wind and the rain and the rumbling in the Creature Clouds, that howling was the only thing you could hear.

Me and Oakley Brownhouse was quiet and kind of frozen in our sodabush.

From his thunderhorse, Astan Loe took a bullhorn and raised it to his mouth.

"CHILDREN," he shouted, "BEFORE YOU STANDS A THIEF AND A MURDERER. HE MUST BE PUNISHED SO THAT OTHERS WILL KNOW THAT THESE ACTIONS WILL NOT BE TOLERATED BY THE SYN-DICATE.

"WHICHEVER ONE OF YOU THROWS THE STONE THAT FELLS OUR CRIMINAL WILL BE

RELEASED FROM YOUR DUTIES IN THE PITS AND IMMEDIATELY INDUCTED INTO THE SYNDICATE AS A FUTURIST. LET THE STONING COMMENCE!"

Then that big blasterbomb-sounding horn blew again and each Digit Kid picked up a rock and *throwed* it at Honeycut. All of the other Syndicate soldiers who was standing in their columns cheered out and pumped their rifles into the air and it seemed like their cheers was the same noise that was rumbling from the Creature Clouds like it was all a bunch of ugly thunder.

The Digit Kids throwed their rocks and when they throwed them their faces looked hard and angry and dead. The Syndicate soldiers holding the tetherchains bucked and swayed as Honeycut tried to moved but he couldn't move.

The rocks hit him everywhere. They hit his stomach and they hit his head and they hit his knees and they hit his neck and he howled out ever louder and he kept howling the same word over and over. Each time the Digit Kids throwed a rock they would bend down and grab another and throw it.

I watched each Digit Kid's face. I ain't sure what I was looking for. It might have been a color or a number on a arm or it might have even been Shale Bluehouse, I don't know. But each face seemed dead to me.

I turnt to Oakley Brownhouse. His eyes looked like they was going to bust right out of his head. His whole body was shaking all fast and electric.

I was like, Go, Oakley Brownhouse! Go now!

He was watching Honeycut all blank and spookfaced.

I went, Don't watch! Just go! and then he scooped up some mud, smashed it over his digits, and he was out of the sodabush and running toward the Syndicate ranks like he was being chased by a gazillion ditch dogs and a gazillion Syndicate soldiers with a gazillion electricity sticks. He was running with my nest outstretched and his other shoe fell off and he almost slipped but he didn't.

Oakley Brownhouse tugged on the tail of the first greatcoat he could reach and this big Syndicate soldier turnt around and Oakley Brownhouse shoved my birthpaper toward him and the Syndicate soldier took it and smoothed it and turnt it away from the rain and read it and then Oakley Brownhouse dropped to the ground and started doing pushups. He did them fast and he did them well and he counted out with each one and you could hear his little Undertwelve voice ringing underneath all the other noises and by the time he had reached twelve two other Syndicate soldiers had turnt around and they was watching too, and it looked like they was kind of laughing at his little naked legs cause of the way they was pointing at them, but Oakley Brownhouse kept pumping off and counting. He made it to eighteen and he made it to nineteen and he even made it to twenty, but I quit watching after that. I quit watching cause I could still hear his little lost voice counting out and I knowed he had made it.

I turnt back to the collection wagon where Honeycut was only half-standing now. The four Syndicate soldiers who was holding the tetherchains had let go and they was just standing there watching with their arms folded. There wasn't too many rocks left but the Digit Kids kept throwing them anyway.

Those Digit Kids' faces never changed. There wasn't nothing but deadness in their little black eyes.

After the black bag fell off of Honeycut's head I tried to not-watch no more, but I couldn't help it. His big blobby face was cut and his cheeks was wet and both of his eyes was black and bloody.

They was doing Honeycut.

They was doing Honeycut on the Today Doubleday.

His body wavered and started to lean and it seemed like he was already dead, but his voice kept howling out.

GIL . . . GIL . . . GIL . . .

CROAKING

You could see the smoke in your breath. The rain was even colder than the night before and I was sure it was going to turn to snow. I still had my plastic and my guts and my thoughts. And all I kept thinking was, Just croak, would you, stupid body! Just croak and get it over with!

I thought if I walked I would croak sooner. I figured that that's how come Joe Painter croaked when he did, cause his croak muscles got excited from building and carrying and leveling the bodybox boat. I figured all that rowing he did in the Red River was the thing that turnt his pee black and made the croak finally come.

I had ice in my feet. They was cold and wet and stiff and I couldn't walk too fast. I stopped puking cause there wasn't nothing left inside but my blood and my bones. Each time I swallowed it felt like I had glass in my throat. That seasick flower in my stomach was climbing right up through my ribs.

I thought about going back and saying goodbye to the Salt Man, but my head felt all light and swervy and I couldn't think too good. Every time I felt myself moving in one direction I would look up and see the same Bone Tree. It was like they was running around again. I tried to stay focused on Elton the Elephant, who was so funny-colored now he looked like he was made that way on purpose. But no matter how hard I tried to stay focused on him the muscles in my brain wouldn't let me find my way.

I heard something crawling toward me. I was hoping it was a big boogywolf or the Slowneck and I wished it would just croak me in one huge monsterglurp. But when I turnt around I seen that it was a ditch dog. It was that same ditch dog with the broken leg that Oakley Brownhouse tried to kick to death. It was crying and its fur was all ratty and it looked like one of his other legs was busted too. It was right there in front of me all muddy and crooked and skinny. Its muzzlestrap was all torn and hanging by a thread. One of its eyes was missing and its tail was bent funny.

When we was a few feet away from each other I started screaming at it.

Croak me! I screamed. *Croak me and get it over with, G!*

It started making these little sissychicken wheezing noises and then it walked away all crooked and tired-looking.

After a while I ate my screams and I just sat down. I didn't cry and I didn't shout and I didn't feel nothing but that seasick flower climbing through my ribcage.

That's when everything started to fade. It felt like this little ghost was floating through my body. I tried to look up and find Elton the Elephant, but the Bone Trees was running and all I could see was the smoke from my breath and the rain sliding through it.

I waked up to seven candles burning. They was yellow and whitehot and their flames was making seven little halos around my bed. Besides the candles everything else was dark and wherever I was smelled like food and candlewax and soap. Seven little shadows was sawing on the walls and when my eyes finally adjusted to the light I could see that there was a woman sitting at the end of the bed. She was wearing a long robe and her head was covered with this hood and her eyes was huge and blue and they was so blue they looked like they would be warm if you touched them.

For a second I thought I was in Croakville or Croaklahoma or wherever God sends you after it's all over, but then I recognized the woman. It was that Babymaker who used to visit Tick Burrowman, the same Babymaker who gave me the plum in the Bone Trees.

She pulled her hood back and her hair was so dark it was like there was secrets hiding in it. Her skin was white and soft-looking and her hands smelled like plants when there was still plants to smell.

I went, Where am I? but she put her finger up to her mouth to shut me up. Then she moved closer and took my hand and when she did I could see that I wasn't wearing no plastic and I wasn't wearing no shoes and I didn't smell like the Red River. I was clean.

I was wearing this big robe. It was the same kind of robe she was wearing and it had a hood and it was soft and smelled like the Bluehouse shower soap from the Holy Family Agency.

The woman folded the sleeves back so she could see my hands and then she took them in hers and held them real soft and gentle. We looked at each other for a long time and it was like we was talking with our eyes. I felt tears in my throat and this ache in my stomach that was so deep it felt like my *feet* was hungry.

She took this warm rag from her pocket and dipped it in a bowl of water next to my bed and she squeezed the rag over my head and all the warm water runned over my face and it felt nice. Every time the Babymaker woman squeezed the warm water over my head I could smell the plants in her hands.

After she squeezed all the water out of the rag she pulled out this little chalkboard and wrote YOU ARE SAFE HERE. Her eyes was smiling and when she opened her mouth her teeth was dim but they was still nice and they didn't take away none of her prettiness. Then she wrote, WHAT'S YOUR NAME?

I was like, Whensday, but then she brought her finger to her lips again and passed me the piece of chalk and I wrote it. I wrote WHENSDAY.

She took the chalk back and wrote, I'M BLUE. I went,

Blue? and she smiled and brought her finger up to her mouth again and I brought my finger up to my mouth and we was quiet.

After a while I wrote, I'M HUNGRY.

She nodded and smiled.

I wrote, GOT ANY BEANS AND FRANKS?

Blue fed me some soup that smelled like salt and eggs and chicken. It was hot and there was a lot of it and it was the best thing I ever ate in my life, I ain't kidding. There was crackers and cheese, too. She spooned me the whole bowl and I dipped the crackers and cheese in the soup and sucked the bits off my fingers and she gave me about five glasses of washed water and when I drinked them I could still feel that seasick flower twisting in my stomach. I could feel its roots and its stem and I could feel the water running down its petals and stuff.

After I finished eating she kissed me on my hair and that felt strange but I kind of liked it. After that she left the room and closed the door behind her. I tried to get up but I was too tired. I wasn't happy and I wasn't sad. I wasn't *nothing*, I think. I wasn't nothing and I didn't think about nothing and then I fell back asleep.

In the Babymakers' life hole there's Quiet and there's Doublequiet. Quiet is the normal kind of silence like when everyone's washing water or writing on chalkboards or making candles. Doublequiet's when there's a warning that someone from the Syndicate is coming. The warning is three loud taps on a chalkboard. During Doublequiet you're supposed to stop what you're doing, stand still, and hold your breath as best you can till someone taps on a chalkboard three times again. There's a Doublequiet warning if a ditch dog comes snuffling by the life hole, too.

This one Lost Man called Seldom Sam keeps lookout. Sometimes you see him in the main room packing cheese or filling his shoulder jug with washed water. He always smiles at me and I like it even though one of his teeth is brown and makes him look like he eats trees.

At first Blue taught me how to roll candles. You got to form the wax around the wick and you got to roll it in these little strips of cheesecloth till it cools. You can make funny shapes like question marks and privacies but Blue don't like that too much. She likes them six inches tall and straight as a comb.

Blue let me roll candles in bed at first cause I was still pretty weak. If I went out into the main room to get a glass of washed water I was so honking tired by the time I got back to my room I thought I wouldn't make it back to my bed. One time I even fell but Seldom Sam was there and he helped me back up and Blue came and put me in my bed.

That went on for a long time—I'm not sure how many doubledays or halfweeks—but I got pretty good at rolling candles. I was warm and dry and my stomach didn't ache no more and my hands started smelling like candlewax.

I stared at the candles and thought about things. I thought about Tick Burrowman and I thought about Honeycut and I thought about Oakley Brownhouse and hoped he was okay. I even thought about Joe Painter and the time we spent on the Red River.

I thought about Shale Bluehouse, too, but my thoughts about him was weak and sad and the muscles in my brain wouldn't let them stick. They just kept getting smaller and smaller the way bugs is small.

One doubleday Blue took her chalkboard and wrote that that thing in my stomach is a baby. She was crying when she wrote it and then she wrote how lucky I was that I didn't lose it when I was running through the Bone Trees. She kept crying on her chalkboard and writing how lucky I was.

At first, having a baby living inside me made me sad cause of how the world is sad. I thought about making myself fall down some stairs. I thought about croaking myself with a rope like Inch Bluestroke. I thought about running into the corner of a table so I could make it pop out of my privacy. I even started punching myself in the guts. But that just made Blue want to strap my arms down with belts and stuff.

At first I couldn't even think of it as a baby. Instead I thought of it as a *duck* or a *chicken*. I even started doing something really stupid and completely ballistic: I started *quacking*. I would walk and quack and waddle but that only got me in trouble again cause of Quiet and Doublequiet and all that chalkboard stuff.

One doubleday I snucked out and walked through the Bone Trees. My stomach was thick and it was starting to stick out and my feet hurt and I felt strange and slow. The trees wasn't running no more. They looked old and tired and they was kind of leaning toward the Red River like they was thirsty. The Creature Clouds was still boiling in the sky but the rain had turnt to snow. The snowflakes was huge and they was almost going sideways and they looked like big paper dolls spinning down.

I wasn't too cold cause my robe was warm and things was cooking inside me. I could feel my boobies growing and I knowed my baby was safe. I was careful not to slip and I had to keep my hood over my head so the snow wouldn't freeze my eyes.

I looked up and I seen Elton the Elephant. He was still at the top of his Bone Tree and he was covered in snow and the whiteness made his trunk and his ears and his tail look even older and sadder than before.

At some point the snow fell slower. It stopped going sideways and it was like cotton floating down and there was a sadness in its slowness. The sky was long and gray and the branches of the Bone Trees looked like they was covered with ashes.

Even though the snow wouldn't stop I was warm. I was warm and my robe felt good against my skin. You can always appreciate those little things. Even if they make you sad you can still appreciate them.